Rebel Glory

To Michelle,
From your
Friend,

LIGHTNING ON ICE SERIES

SERIES

Rebel Glory

SIGMUND BROUWER

WORD PUBLISHING
Dallas·London·Vancouver·Melbourne

For Peter Anholt—
the Rebels will never have
a better coach.

REBEL GLORY

Copyright © 1995 by Sigmund Brouwer.

All rights reserved. No portion of this book may be
reproduced in any form without the written
permission of the publisher, except for
brief excerpts in reviews.

Managing Editor: Laura Minchew
Project Editor: Beverly Phillips

Library of Congress Cataloging–in–Publication Data

Brouwer, Sigmund, 1959–
    Rebel glory / Sigmund Brouwer.
        p.   cm.—(Lightning on ice series; 1)
    "Word kids!"
        Summary: Seventeen-year-old hockey star B. T. McPhee needs
to figure out why his team is suddenly being victimized by a series
of mysterious accidents which threaten their chances to win the
playoffs.
    ISBN 0–8499–3637–3
    [1. Hockey—Fiction.   2. Conduct of life—Fiction.   3. Mystery
and detective stories.]   I. Title.   II. Series: Brouwer, Sigmund,
1959–   Lightning on ice series; 1.
PZ7.B79984Re   1995
[Fic]—dc20   95–19383
                                                                              CIP
                                                                              AC

Printed in the United States of America
96 97 98 99 00   QBP   9 8 7 6 5 4

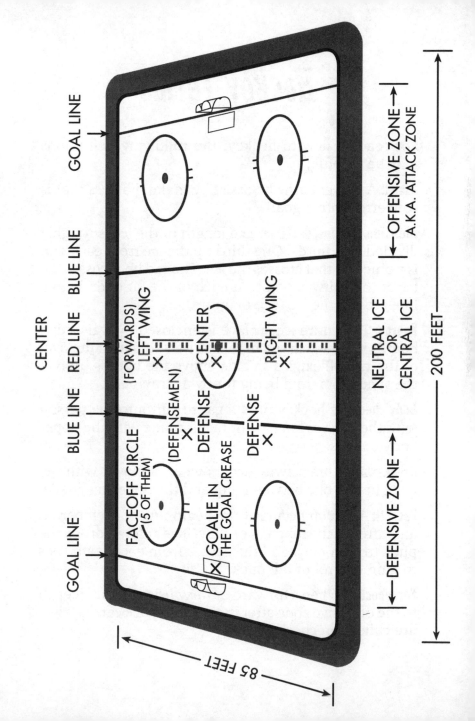

Hockey Terms

For readers new to hockey, the following definitions may be helpful.

Assist: A player earns an assist by making a pass that is converted into a goal.

Blue line, red line, goal line: The length of the ice is roughly divided into thirds. One third up the ice from each end is a blue line that crosses the ice. The red line crosses the ice at the halfway point. At each of the far ends, a goal line crosses the ice (see diagram).

Boards: The entire ice surface is enclosed by waist-high boards that are curved in the corners to match the oval of the rink. Plexiglas shields above the boards protect the spectators from being hit by a stray puck.

Body check: In hockey, it is legal to run into the person with the puck as long as contact is made with the upper body or hips.

Breakaway: A breakaway occurs when a player with the puck has no one between him and the opposing goalie.

Faceoff: A faceoff occurs at the beginning of each period and after each stoppage of play. The referee drops the puck to start play, and the center from each team tries to gain control of the puck.

Forechecker: When a forward or forwards are sent deep in to the offensive zone after the puck or puck carrier, they are called forecheckers.

Hipcheck: A hipcheck is similar to a body check except contact is made as the hip is swung outward.

Icing: An icing penalty is called when a player shoots from behind his blue line and the puck travels all the way across the goal line at the far end. It results in a faceoff in the player's own end, which cancels the advantage of having moved the puck so far.

One-time: The process of hitting the puck without first stopping it.

Overtime: Overtime rules vary in different leagues. In the WHL, it consists of ten minutes of extra play. The first team to score in the extra time wins the game (called sudden-death overtime). In regular season play, a tie at the end of overtime remains a tie. In playoff games, overtime is played until a goal is scored to break the tie.

Period: A regular hockey game consists of sixty minutes of play, divided into three twenty-minute periods.

Point: (1) A single point is given for a goal. (2) In team standings, zero points are accumulated for a loss, one point for a tie, and two points for a win. (3) When a defenseman is standing inside the opposition's blue line, his position is also referred to as "standing at the point."

Power play: Penalties in hockey result in the offending player "serving time" in the penalty box. This time varies according to the penalty. With one and sometimes two fewer players on the ice, the penalized team is at a tremendous disadvantage. The unpenalized team is then considered to be on the power play. It is also known as a "man advantage" or a "two-man advantage."

Slap shot: A slap shot is the hardest shot in hockey. A player raises his stick above his shoulders before swinging downward to "slap" the shot. Slap shots have been recorded at speeds of well over 100 miles per hour.

Stickhandle: Controlling the puck by moving it from side to side with the blade of the hockey stick.

Two-on-one, three-on-one, four-on-one, etc.: If there is only one defenseman between the goalie and two attackers with the puck, it is called a "two-on-one"; the other numbers correspond to the various situations.

One

With the referee dropping the puck at center ice to start the game, my defense partner, Jason Mulridge, decided to lose not only his mind but also much of his hockey equipment.

Only two months had passed since I had been traded to play defense for the Red Deer Rebels. In that time I had learned to expect great hockey moves from Jason. I had watched him stickhandle* while sliding on his knees. I had admired the way he hipchecked* guys from out of nowhere. And I had been dazzled once to see him score with two guys wrapped around his shoulders. In my twenty-five games since joining this team in January, I had learned to expect nearly anything from number 33.

But nothing in those twenty-five games had prepared me for the hockey move Jason was now making on the blue line* beside me.

---

* An asterisk in the text indicates a hockey term that is in the list
   of definitions on pages vi–viii.

The ref had his back to Jason and had just dropped the puck. As I glanced sideways to see if my defense partner was ready, Jason threw his gloves and stick high into the air.

"Are you nuts?" I yelled to be heard above the screaming of five thousand unfriendly fans. *Is he pulling off his gloves to fight? But who does he want to fight with?*

Jason didn't reply. His glove did though. It landed on my helmet and bounced to the ice. The other glove thunked down beside Jason. His stick slid across the ice toward me.

"Are you nuts?" I yelled again. The fans roared louder at Jason's actions. We were in Lethbridge to play the Hurricanes, and their crowd was always tough on us. We didn't need this to make it worse. Not when it was one of the most important games left in the season.

Jason ignored me. He threw his helmet off and yanked his sweater over his head. It exposed his shoulder pads, the white skin of his thick arms, and a torn black T-shirt.

Ahead of us, the two center-ice men were fighting for control. The Hurricane center managed to kick the puck ahead, and it slid toward Jason.

Jason? He was still dancing at the blue line.

It seemed to happen all at once. Jason threw his sweater toward me. It flew into my face like a blanket in the wind. I pulled it away from my eyes just in time to see the Hurricane right winger move in on the puck and sweep past Jason. The Hurricane center was close behind and skating around me. I took a step forward to stop them, but my skate landed on Jason's stick, and I skidded to my knees. The rest of our guys were too far away to catch up.

Jason was still on the blue line, grabbing at the nylon belt which held up his hockey pants. *Great. Two guys around us and swooping down on our goalie, and Jason is still undressing.*

The crowd's roar thundered. Maybe at the breakaway* on our goalie. Maybe at Jason. Probably at both.

On my knees, I was too stunned to stand, too stunned to yell at Jason again. A couple of our guys had stopped. The referee's whistle had fallen from his mouth, and he stared at Jason.

Jason had finally gotten the belt strap undone and pulled his belt loose.

At the same time, the Hurricane winger went left to pull our goalie out of position and slid the puck across to the center. He snapped a shot into the open right side of our net.

Jason rammed his pants down to his ankles.

I couldn't believe it. We were down 1–0 less than ten seconds into the game. In the same time, my partner was down to his red long johns and his hockey socks.

Jason didn't stop there either.

He leaned over and pulled at the garters of his right sock. He tugged until the garters finally slipped loose. He peeled his sock down and pulled his plastic shin pad from the sock.

By then, no one on the ice was moving. The fans were so loud I wondered if the fillings in my teeth would shake loose. And Coach Blair was standing on top of the boards* at our bench, shaking his fist at Jason.

Jason had the right shin pad loose and in his hands. He straightened and threw the shin pad as far as he could.

We all watched that pad sail through the air. It sailed so long that everyone at the ice rink had time to stare and wonder. It sailed so long that the crowd's roar became silence.

What seemed like minutes later, the shin pad fell to the ice, almost at the other blue line. And when it landed, we understood why Jason had gone crazy.

Four or five cockroaches exploded from the inside of his shin pad, scurrying in all directions on the ice. *Cockroaches.* Those big, black, ugly bugs so gross they make beetles look cuddly. *Cockroaches.* Trying to find someplace to hide on the ice around them.

One of the Hurricane defensemen slammed his stick down and nailed two of them. With the crowd still silent, we heard the crunch as the stick broke the hard shells. Bug juice sprayed like tobacco juice.

Jason struggled to roll his other sock down. When he did, same result. A high-flying shin pad and cockroaches scattering in all directions when it hit the ice.

Just as if someone had punched the play button on a CD player, the crowd's roar returned, louder than before.

I noticed a few cockroaches crawling near Jason's skates. These must have spilled from inside his hockey pants. As Jason tore at his shoulder pads, he stepped on one of the cockroaches, popping it like a cherry tomato. More bug juice sprayed.

4

The crowd kept roaring, and Jason now had his shoulder pads off. A single cockroach dropped from the shoulder pads and landed between his skates.

Jason threw the shoulder pads and, without waiting for them to land, peeled off his torn black T-shirt.

I nearly lost the hamburgers I had eaten a couple hours earlier. At least three cockroaches were crawling on Jason's belly, their antennas quivering in all directions.

Jason looked down, saw the cockroaches on him, screamed, and fainted. It put him flat on his back on the ice. He lay there as the trainer came running from the player's bench.

Those of us on the ice leaned on our sticks as we watched the trainer prop Jason into a sitting position. The trainer waved smelling salts beneath Jason's nose.

"McPhee," I heard a voice say beside me. I turned my head to look into the eyes of the Hurricane center who had just scored on us.

"Yeah?" I shouted above the crowd.

"Bad scene with these cockroaches, McPhee," he said. He shook his head sadly from side to side. "Don't you guys ever shower?"

Two

We were down three goals by the end of the first period*, something Coach Blair did not find amusing.

"Three to nothing!" he shouted as we filed into the dressing room at the end of the period. "Three to nothing! This game is worth four points* and all of you are skating like ballerinas out there!"

Coach Blair was right about the four points . . . and about skating like ballerinas.

Two months ago, we had been in last place in the league and seventeen points out of the playoffs. Right now, we were only seven points out and chasing the Hurricanes hard for the final playoff position in our division. If we could win this game, we would stop the Hurricanes from taking two points, and we would gain those two points for ourselves. Four very big points. Winning would put us only five points behind them. But losing would mean we'd be nine points back. There wasn't much time left in the season to recover.

I looked around the dressing room at the other nineteen

guys sitting on the benches. I didn't know many of them too well. It takes me a while to make friends. I did know, however, that they could have played better. Much better.

"Burnell!" Coach Blair shouted at the guy beside me. "What's your excuse?"

Hog Burnell lifted his head. He had been staring at the floor, hoping not to be noticed. But it's pretty tough not to notice someone like Hog. Big, wide, and with a squashed nose that had been broken at least three times, he had a crew cut so short his skull reflected the lights. The program listed his first name as Timothy, but I had never heard anyone call him that.

"Aw, Coach," Hog said, "I kept thinking cockroaches were crawling through my equipment."

At any other time, we might have found Hog's excuse funny.

Not now, though. Coach Blair—all six feet two inches of him—was red-faced with anger. But if the guys were thinking what I was thinking, we all shared Hog's fear.

"What?" Coach Blair has a face that looks like it was carved from the side of a mountain. When he glares, you want to take cover. "Explain yourself!"

Hog gulped. "Well, Coach, every time I felt sweat trickle down my back, I wondered if it was a cockroach. I mean, Jason . . ."

I looked across at Jason. He was dressed in his equipment again, but he hadn't played a good first period. All three goals had been scored on his side of the defense. His eyes were wide as Hog mentioned the cockroaches.

"B. T.!" Coach Blair yelled. "How about you?"

B. T. meant me. Brian Thomas McPhee. Number 3.

Seventeen years old and an all-star defenseman here in the Western Hockey League. I was traded from the Brandon Wheat Kings to the Red Deer Rebels. And I hoped to be a high draft pick into the National Hockey League, a dream that filled my sleep nearly every night.

"Coach," I said, "I kept wondering if I had bugs in my equipment, too."

Coach Blair kicked the garbage can in the center of the dressing room.

"All of you," he shouted, "peel down! Shake out your equipment. Prove to yourselves there are no cockroaches on you. You've got ten minutes before the next period starts."

Even though I'd never seen him lose his temper like this, I guessed why it was happening now—newspapers.

Coach Blair's job was on the line. At least that's what the newspapers said. His only chance to keep his job was to get the Red Deer Rebels into the playoffs. That was the main reason I was here—to help a shaky defense system.

"Coach, why didn't the ref blow the whistle during the first play?" I asked as the team stripped. "I mean, any time the gloves are off, the ref's supposed to stop play."

"I asked him about that," Coach Blair said. His face was still red with anger. "He said he didn't see Jason's gloves on the ice until the breakaway was already happening. By then it was too late. He couldn't take the breakaway from them."

He glared as the team shook out its gear. "When this

game's over, we will discuss what happened to Jason. I can promise you right now if one of you was behind it, you're off the team."

That had crossed my mind too. How could so many cockroaches have gotten into Jason's equipment? How could they have stayed hidden while he was dressing? And why just Jason? This was as weird as anything I'd heard of in hockey.

"Hey, bud," I whispered to Jason as Coach Blair stomped out of the dressing room. "Didn't you feel those cockroaches during warm-up?"

He shook his head. "Coach Blair asked me that too. I was skating and shooting during warm-up, and I didn't notice anything. I itched a little when we stood during the national anthem. Then I felt something moving all over me and . . ."

I shook my head in sympathy.

"Even though I knew the game was ready to start, I couldn't help myself," he finished. "I felt things moving all around beneath my equipment, and I went crazy. Ever since I was a kid I've hated bugs. This was like my worst nightmare."

"You all right now?" I asked him.

Around us, the players were pulling off shoulder pads, elbow pads, and shin pads. They were banging the equipment against the floor and benches. Not a single cockroach fell into sight. Jason had been the only one attacked by cockroaches.

"All right?" he repeated. "All right? The only thing that will make this all right is if we win the game."

Three

We didn't win the game. Worse, the score wasn't even close. Mr. Palmer, my high school English teacher, was only too happy to remind me about this on Monday morning back in Red Deer.

"What happened in Lethbridge against the Hurricanes, McPhee?" Mr. Palmer smirked at me from the front of the classroom. "Did you find out you can't count on being a hockey hero all your life?"

Mr. Palmer was completely bald with caterpillar eyebrows. He had a nose so long you could land an airplane on it. His teeth and fingers were stained yellow from smoking cigarettes all the time.

Mr. Palmer didn't like me much, mainly because on my first day in class, I had made the mistake of arguing with him. I can easily remember that morning.

Cheryl Holbrook, the girl sitting in the desk beside me, had dropped a book from her backpack. Mr. Palmer had glared at her for interrupting him, and then he had noticed the book on the floor—a Bible.

"You don't believe in those fairy tales, do you?" Mr. Palmer had asked with a mean laugh.

"They're not fairy—" She tried to finish, but Mr. Palmer didn't give her a chance.

"Only fools buy into that stuff," he said, "especially when history shows what terrible things churches have done. And look at some of today's television preachers. Pretty tough to believe when faced with people like that, wouldn't you say?"

I could see Cheryl's face turn red. I guessed from anger, not embarrassment. She didn't seem like a wallflower. Mr. Palmer glared at her, daring her to speak. Stupidly, I opened my mouth before Cheryl could say anything.

"Actually, sir," I said, "logically, that is a very dumb argument."

Mr. Palmer's caterpillar eyebrows swung in my direction. "What?!" He sounded like he couldn't believe someone would disagree with him. Especially someone on his first day in class.

It was too late to shut my mouth now. My dad had been a lawyer before he died. He had always tried to get me to use logic.

"Wouldn't you say the church and the preachers are just delivering a message?" I asked. "That they are messengers?"

"So?" Mr. Palmer said.

"A messenger is not the message. The message and the messenger are two different things, whether it's a newspaper story or a speech from a politician or from a preacher. What's true about the messenger doesn't

11

also have to be true about the message. Just because some television preachers are idiots, doesn't mean their message is stupid."

— I think Dad would have been proud of how I'd argued my point. I was also rewarded by a big smile from Cheryl Holbrook. It was a smile worth working for.

Mr. Palmer wasn't proud at all. Or happy. Mr. Palmer's eyeballs bulged out like a constipated frog's.

"Your name?" he finally demanded.

— "Brian McPhee."

He stared at me for a few moments. "The new hockey player? Are you too stupid to know that all hockey players are stupid?"

"That is another dumb argument," I said. On the outside I may have seemed calm, but inside I was boiling. "All I have to do is find one smart hockey player to prove your argument wrong." I paused and smiled. "Sir."

"Good luck finding one smart hockey player," he said. "Unless you're going to call yourself smart."

I couldn't understand why he had such an attitude. Most teachers did their best to help hockey players because most of the players wanted education *and* hockey, and doing both was tough without support from the teachers. Anyway, my first two years in junior hockey had shown me there were better things to be afraid of than someone like this, attitude or not.

"Is that how you win arguments, sir?" I asked. "By being a bully to students who can't really fight back?"

"That's enough out of you," he yelled. "You can leave the classroom!"

I smiled at him again. "I guess you just proved my point," I said as I gathered my books.

That's how my first day in his English class had ended. Since then, Mr. Palmer had been doing his best to make my life tough. So the morning after losing the cockroach game to the Hurricanes was not a good time to be sitting in Mr. Palmer's class.

He repeated his question. "Hey, McPhee? Did you find out you can't count on being a hockey hero all your life?"

It wouldn't do any good to say that I had scored both of our team's goals. "There's always next game, sir."

He hated it when I called him sir.

"Next game? You guys don't have a chance. The Winter Hawks are in first place. They'll kill you."

For someone who hated hockey so much, he sure kept close track of what happened in the Western Hockey League. I knew why, too. I'd heard he once wanted to play pro, and he was good enough to do it. But he was afraid of getting hurt, so he never made it. Maybe it was easier to be mad at us instead of himself.

"We have a chance," I said.

"Tell you what," he said. "If you guys win, the entire class gets a free day. No English lessons. But if you lose," he added, "you . . ." He thought for a few seconds, his caterpillar eyebrows moving up and down.

Then he smiled a nasty smile that showed too many yellow teeth. "If the Rebels lose, McPhee, you sing 'Mary Had a Little Lamb' over the intercom to the entire school."

"You have a deal," I said. "And we won't lose."

 *Four*

When we stepped onto the ice to play the Portland
Winter Hawks, I had more to worry about than singing
a stupid nursery rhyme over the high school intercom.
We really needed to win this game to keep the Hurricanes
from getting too far ahead of us in the standings. Not
only that, we had heard there would be a Boston Bruins
scout in the stands. This close to making it to the
National Hockey League, you hated to make mistakes.

The first two and a half periods went better than we
could have hoped. We were actually up 3–2. All we had
to do was hang on to the lead for the final nine minutes
of the game.

The Red Deer crowd really got into the game, which
made it more fun for us. The Centrium is one of the
newest arenas in the league, and when it has a full house,
a close game seems like a Stanley Cup playoff final.

Rowdy, the Rebels' mascot, was a guy in a deer
costume with dark glasses and big brown antlers.
Rowdy was having fun too. Little kids followed him

from section to section in the stands. He had the fans cheering and clapping and hollering.

——Then I heard a different yell from behind me.

"Scum sucking hosebags!" It takes a lot to snap me away from the game, but this guy sounded like a shot moose.

I turned my head slightly to look. Yes, it was stupid. Coach Blair says never let the fans get to you. If they notice that you're noticing them, they'll keep yelling all the way into next year.

But this guy was as bad as a foghorn. A fat foghorn with a round face and a wart on the end of his nose. He yelled so loud most of us on the bench turned around and looked up—just in time to see him dump cola on me from a huge plastic cup. The cola splashed across my helmet and shoulders.

The crowd noise grew as some nearby fans noticed. Our assistant coach yelled for security. The guys down the bench screamed. And above all of this noise, I heard it.

"B. T.!"

Jewels Larken, our backup goalie, yelled again. "B. T.! Incoming!"

Incoming meant a shift change without waiting for the whistle to stop play.

With cola dripping down the visor of my helmet, I hopped over the boards. My skates were moving even before I touched the ice. As I cut to cover my position at the far side of the ice, I tried to catch the flow of the play. Unfortunately, ducking the cola had taken my eyes from the game. It took me several seconds to figure out what was happening.

15

I went into my mental checklist of all the players on the ice. It was a way for me to make time seem slower. It was also a way to keep me from feeling panic, something that was always much closer to me than anyone knew.

Their right defenseman had the puck behind their net. Check. *Their other defenseman was in front of their net.* Check. *Their center was swooping in from my left to go behind their net and pick up the puck.* Check. *Hog, our left winger, was chasing their center and going deep as the single forechecker*.* Check. *So far so good. Their right winger was already in motion at the blue line and straddling it as he cut straight across toward me.* Check. *We needed our center to fill the gap at the top of their faceoff circle and block the up-ice pass. . . . No center! Where was Mancini at center? And where was Shertzer to cover the winger ahead of me?*

My checklist was blown to shreds.

Maybe it had happened because of the cola thrown at me—Mancini and Shertzer had tangled while trying to get onto the ice. For the few seconds it took them to unscramble, we were on the wrong end of a five-on-three.*

Their left defenseman busted straight up the ice toward me. Their right defenseman took advantage of the confusion by stepping out from behind the net and firing a long pass up the middle. He hit their right winger, who was already in full stride and suddenly a step ahead of my partner, Jason.

And just like that, in the flip of a heartbeat, they had the three-on-one*, leaving behind Jason and Hog, with Mancini and Shertzer still trying to clear the players' bench.

It was only me against their two wingers and left defenseman.

Their right winger cut up the ice toward me with the puck. Their left winger hugged the boards to draw me toward him. Their defenseman trailed the play.

I skated backward as they moved on me like a trio of sharks. A part of me felt the roar of the crowd. Another part saw Mancini and Shertzer finally on their feet and skating hard to catch up. But I knew I'd be alone. In this league, you can't give anyone a head start, least of all the Winter Hawks.

Now I was inside our blue line. I had my hockey stick in my left hand and pointed at one guy. I held my right hand at chest level, pointing at another to remind myself of their positions.

Stay even with me guys, I silently pleaded to them. *Make the mistake of letting me keep the middle.*

Only in my wildest dreams. They made no mistakes. The puck handler cut wide, the other winger dropped, and their trailing defenseman crisscrossed.

Now I had to make a choice. Should I guard against the pass and let the puck handler go in alone . . . or lose a half step to stay with the puck handler and set him up for a wide-open drop pass, with another guy busting in to pull our goalie in two directions.

I hesitated and that made my choice. The guy with the puck somehow found another burst of speed and pumped past me. That mistake left me with only one choice. I had to go for the puck, not cover a pass.

I spun and dove.

All my eyes registered was the puck. If I could sweep

it first, I could follow through and no ref would call it tripping. But if I missed the puck and tangled with the winger's skates . . . penalty shot.

— My breath bounced from my lungs as I strained and . . . bingo!

Even above the roar of the crowd, I heard the thunk of my stick blade against hard rubber, and the puck slid harmlessly into the corner. Then his skates bit into the shaft of my stick and he fell down on top of me. We both tumbled into the goalie and net. The sweet shrillness of the whistle reached my ears to end the play.

When something like that happens, you don't feel the bruises until the next day. Especially when your team-mates help you to your feet and pound your back in glee.

I'd stopped a crucial three-on-one late in the game. The Boston Bruins' scout had to have noticed.

But my herohood only lasted another seven minutes and sixteen seconds of electronic scoreboard time. Because that's how much time passed before I was last man back at our blue line, back-pedaling and stickhandling the puck as I got ready to pass it by their center and ahead to Hog Burnell.

It was a play I could make a thousand times blindfolded. Only this time, as I made a backward turn, I lost my balance and slammed onto my backside. It was such a hard and unexpected fall that my helmet crashed against the ice.

Their center scooped up the puck and blew past me. I didn't even have time to try to trip him. There I was, alone and flat on my back as the Winter Hawk center scored the game-tying goal in front of 6,200 fans.

The only good thing was that we didn't lose in overtime*. But we didn't win either. The scored remained tied, 3–3. We only earned a single point in a race to make the playoffs.

I knew my mistake had taken the win away from us. I had also played horrible in overtime, falling at least once every shift on the ice. After the game, I showered in miserable silence, alone in a crowded dressing room.

When I left the dressing room, I was still alone. Instead of heading for the parking lot and my old pickup truck, I walked into the stands. My steps echoed in the emptiness of the arena.

Barely an hour earlier, our team had lived and died with each shot on the net. Now the lights were dim, the scoreboard dark, the ice shiny and quiet.

Anyone watching might have decided I was trying to figure out how I had managed to trip over my own skates. Unfortunately, I already had the answer to that.

On my left skate, one of the rivets that held the blade to the boot had been removed. Another rivet had loosened itself during the game. It hadn't loosened enough to move the blade much. But it was enough to wobble me when I least expected it—enough to make me fall when I made a sharp turn.

I wasn't sitting alone in the stands trying to figure out why I had fallen. I was wondering who would have removed the rivet. And why.

Five

"**S**ure I can see the rivet is gone." Teddy shrugged. "But that's a long stretch from saying someone actually took the rivet out."

I hadn't slept too well after last night's game. Nor had I been able to keep my mind on school during the day. Still, there was one good thing. Our tie meant I didn't have to sing over the intercom. Now it was an hour before practice, and I had found Teddy, our trainer, in the team dressing room at the arena.

Teddy was short, as if years and years of road trips and dressing rooms had pounded him down to his solid, chunky shape. He had straggly gray hair, a gray mustache, and ears that stuck out like handles on a teacup.

"And remember that guy who threw cola," I said. "He couldn't have picked a worse time. Guys coming off the ice. Guys trying to get on the ice. Maybe it wasn't an accident. And maybe Jason's cockroaches weren't an accident. You've got to admit that was strange too. All of this is hurting us on the scoreboard."

He shook his head. "B. T., you've got some kinda imagination. Maybe you should stop reading all them books on the bus."

"Come on," I said, handing him my skate. "Look at the plastic where the rivet was. See where it's rough?"

He held the skate up to the light and squinted at the plastic. After a few minutes, he handed it back to me.

"You got a point. Those could be snip marks from a pair of pliers or cutters."

"I told you."

He put up his hand to stop me before I got too wound up. "And they could easily *not* be snip marks but just banged up plastic. That happens, too, you know." Teddy rubbed a dirty hand across his stubbled chin. "Maybe you dropped them a couple times and knocked the rivet off."

"This is me," I reminded him. "I don't drop skates."

He laughed. "You're right. Not the kid the news-hounds have nicknamed 'Computer.'"

He grinned some more, showing broken teeth. Teddy had been—as he would often tell us—a goalie in the old days. Before protective face masks.

He continued, "*Computer.* Me and the boys got a bet going. Next time a puck or skate cuts you, we figure ice water's gonna come out of your veins instead of blood."

"My skates, Teddy . . ." I didn't like hearing about the bet. I'd worked hard all season to make sure no one

21

knew about the panic that I felt every time I laced on skates. Brains will overcome the panic, I'd told myself again and again. Dad had always said that brains would overcome most any problem.

And if people wanted to believe I had no fear, I'd gladly let them. But what would happen if the panic finally struck and I couldn't play high-pressure hockey anymore? Would I still be able to stand in this team dressing room and shoot the breeze with a trainer who had seen everything in fifty-odd years of hockey?

There were practice jerseys piled in one corner, ready for laundry. Lockers stood half-open—no one needed to worry about theft on this team. Equipment was hanging everywhere with the hope it might be dry before practice this afternoon. The smell of old sweat and new sweat mixed with the welcome sharp spearmint of the muscle ointment we all used. Sticks leaned against one wall. A chalkboard hung on the other.

This room was the inner workings of Junior A hockey, something every one on the team had fought for years to reach. I didn't want it taken away from me because I suddenly fell apart on the ice and began to play like an idiot. And I didn't want anyone to know about my fear of playing like an idiot.

So I pointed again at the blade and repeated myself. "Rivets, Teddy. One snipped off and the other loosened."

"Yeah, yeah," he said. "So maybe I might agree this damage got done on purpose. Then what?"

I stared at him. "Then what? Then we protest to the league or something. I don't know. But it isn't fair that—"

"B. T.," he told me, "we all saw you fall. It cost us a win. Stuff happens."

I held up my skate.

Teddy made a snorting noise. "You gonna get the skates checked for fingerprints?"

I felt myself flush.

"Look," Teddy said. "You're a big, good-looking kid. Not real dumb. And a great player. The world's ahead of you. If you run around putting the blame on other people, you'll get a bad name. People don't like whiners. That might be enough to keep you out of pro."

How could it be whining when it just wasn't fair that someone wrecked my skate? I opened my mouth to argue, but I saw the hard look on Teddy's face and snapped my mouth shut.

He noticed me change my mind. He patted me on the shoulder. "You learn quick, kid. That's what I like about you. Keep your mouth shut and play hard. Tomorrow night's game in the Hat will give you a chance to make up for last night. In the meantime, leave your skates with me, and I'll be sure they get fixed."

Then he flicked on the grinder and bent over to sharpen a skate blade against the granite wheel. I took the hint that he was finished talking to me.

As I walked away, I decided I would keep my mouth shut. No sense in looking like a whiner. But I had a few questions I wanted answered. So while I kept my mouth shut, I'd make sure I kept my eyes and ears wide open.

Six

Mighty Ducks—the movie, not the NHL team—filled the television screen, and most of the guys groaned at the funny spots, which was a good indication of how many times we had seen it during our road trips on this bus.

Groans or not, being able to watch videos on the bus was one of the great things about playing in the WHL. Especially compared to road trips in the leagues we played in when we were younger. In those days, a road trip meant long hours on a beat-up, creaking, groaning bus. Night was the worst, when the passing countryside was just a blur of darkness broken by occasional farm lights.

But in this league, the long distances went a lot quicker. We rode a luxury bus with plenty of room to stretch and with a television and VCR mounted high at the front of the aisle. Good thing too. This trip to Medicine Hat to play the Tigers took more than four hours. And the Tigers were one of the closer teams to Red Deer.

Usually I ignored the video movies and lost myself in books—mysteries, sports, you name it. I would often be surprised to look up and discover we had arrived. Today, though, I couldn't concentrate on reading, not with the folded newspaper under my seat.

So I groaned along with everyone else when Coach Blair stood and reached up to push the on/off button of the television. Coach Blair was a big man who looked even bigger and tougher in his dark navy double-breasted suit. His short brown hair had streaks of gray already, although his bio sheet said he was still in his thirties. When he grinned, his face stopped looking like it was a chunk of mountain. But when he frowned, it looked like the mountain was going to fall on you.

He wasn't smiling now.

"Save your groans for the trip back," Coach Blair said as the screen went black, "because if I don't get a hundred and ten percent from every player tonight, you can expect a double practice tomorrow."

We shut up.

He let his eyes travel up and down the aisle, looking each of us square in the face before he spoke again. "You've all seen the newspaper."

More than a few players looked around to see what I might do. Jason Mulridge and Hog Burnell came closer to being my friends than anyone on the team. Those two had made a point of showing anger at the newspaper article. A few others had half-nodded in agreement. The

25

rest had said and done nothing. Which shows that trouble is a quick way to figure out who is on your side and who isn't.

Coach Blair made a point of not looking at me as he spoke. He held up a copy of the same paper I had beneath my seat. "I do not, repeat, do not believe what they're writing about us in the local paper," he said. "We're going to prove them utterly wrong. This team is not a team of chokers. We will *not* fold under pressure. And when all of you skate hard, *nobody* beats us."

He waved the folded newspaper at us. "I'm not saying beat the Tigers tonight or else. They're a tough team on home ice. And sometimes games are decided by bad refs or a wrong bounce—nothing you can prevent. But if we lose because we get lazy, you can expect to skate till you throw up in tomorrow's practice."

He stared hard, waiting to see if anyone dared to comment.

We didn't.

"Good," he finished. "Now start thinking about the game."

In the silence that followed, broken only by the humming of the bus tires, I tried to follow Coach Blair's instructions. But I couldn't. Not with his reminder about the newspaper article.

In the same way you can't resist lifting a bandage to check a new set of stitches, I had to see the newspaper again. I pulled it out from under my seat, even though I knew what I would see.

The headline said "Folding Act Begins Again?" No

matter how I tried, I could find nothing good in a single sentence.

Folding Act Begins Again?

History, it is said, has a habit of repeating itself. It appears the Red Deer Rebels are doing their best to prove the saying true.

It was almost a year ago that the Rebels were ready to sweep through the final third of the season with an excellent shot at finishing first in the division. Instead, the team went into a tailspin that dumped them so low in division standings they had to climb just to reach the basement.

It was no surprise then that the Rebels stayed in last place for the first third of this season. The real surprise has come in the last two months, when they started winning again, giving us hope they might reach the playoffs. Much or most of the credit for that belongs to the defensive steadiness of Brian McPhee, obtained from the Brandon Wheat Kings because of his reputation as a player who gets better as the pressure is added. McPhee is the efficient player who has so little flash and makes so few mistakes that you suspect he is a computer on skates.

That is why it hurt so much to see him—of all people—choke during the final minutes of a crucial game against the Winter Hawks. McPhee, all alone with the puck at his own blue line, gave up a breakaway. Result? Winter Hawk goal. Winter Hawk tie. And only one point instead of a much-needed two.

There are other signs of trouble too. Players running into each other as they leave the box. Needless penalties. Missed open nets. Little things. But taken together, they may point to big disaster. And can anyone explain why Jason Mulridge stripped himself of equipment before the game against the Lethbridge Hurricanes? That did not help the team either.

Is this the beginning of another nightmare collapse for the Rebels? Will our season again end with stands only a quarter full of fans who have more to boo than cheer?

Let us hope not.

These kids have shown us they really can win games. If they decide not to choke, they will be contenders. And if they do choke, they will discover how quickly diamonds can turn to dust. While it is up to all of them, one way or the other, McPhee will be the one to set the example.

If they do not win, it might be time to say good-bye to Coach Blair. And if the team is purchased by someone from out of town, we might also end up saying good-bye to the entire Rebel team. Of course, if they do another folding act, we might not miss them anyway.

I set the paper down and stared out the window at the open fields of the flat prairie north of Medicine Hat.

My highly depressing thoughts were interrupted when I felt my teeth rattle.

"Hey," someone shouted. "A flat tire!"

A roaring flap-flap-flap of rubber against the wheel wells slowed, then stopped as the bus driver pulled over and parked on the shoulder.

Coach Blair yelled for attention. "Go outside for a break if you want. But stay in the ditch. Anyone goes near the road, I'll kill him quicker than any passing truck could."

For an early March day, it was warm. Most of us decided not to bother with our jackets. Here, a couple hours south of Red Deer, the Alberta fields held no snow. The breeze moving from those dirt-brown fields carried the smell of spring. It felt good to stretch and pull in lungfuls of fresh air.

The bus driver already had a back hatch of the bus

open, and pieces of a huge tire jack sat on the pavement beside him.

I wandered over to watch.

"I can't believe this," the bus driver was muttering to Coach Blair.

Coach Blair shrugged. "That's why we always leave in plenty of time. In case the bus breaks down."

"But these tires are new," the bus driver said. "This one shouldn't have shredded."

I caught them looking at me, so I hunched my shoulders and turned away. Last thing I wanted was a coach-to-player chat from Coach Blair about how he was sure I would play better tonight. If he started talking to me that way, it would be all I could do not to make excuses and tell him about my skate rivets.

It took a half hour to change the tire. That, as Coach Blair announced, would still let us arrive forty-five minutes before game time. Except a little farther down the road, the spare tire went too. Did I want to believe both flat tires were accidents?

Yes.

Could I? No. Cockroaches in Jason's equipment. Someone in our home crowd throwing cola on us at the worst moment. My skate rivet removed. Now two tires blown on the same trip. If someone was trying to make sure we didn't play our best hockey, that someone was doing a good job. Our team made it to the Medicine Hat arena only twenty minutes before the puck would be dropped to start the game.

Seven

"**M**ove! Move! Move!" Teddy shouted in the dressing room in Medicine Hat. Teddy's face was red and the little veins on his nose looked like wriggle worms. "Hurry! Hurry! Hurry!"

Coach Blair moved beside him. "They're doing the best they can," he said. "No sense making it worse."

Teddy took a breath and calmed himself. "But you said we didn't want to delay the game. And opening face off is any minute and—"

"Teddy, they're doing their best," Coach Blair repeated. "These kids are already nervous enough."

We were.

I probably wasn't supposed to overhear their conversation, but I was sitting on the dressing room bench closest to them. I was already dressed in my hockey gear and only had to tie my skates, giving me time to look around.

The dressing room was a mess. Some of the guys had

been in so much of a hurry that their street clothes were in heaps on the floor. Others were shouting for their sticks. Or tape. Or equipment adjustments.

Jason Mulridge caught my eye. He winked, as if to say, "What's the big deal?" Jason, the guy with the face all the girls in high school wanted to smother with kisses, was so cool. The only time I'd seen him rattled was the cockroach incident. Jason, like me, had also dressed quickly enough that he only needed to tie his skates. And like me, he preferred to keep his skates loose for as long as possible and always undid them between periods. Your feet get plenty of punishment during the game. No sense making it worse by keeping them tight during rests.

"Three minutes left," Coach Blair said quietly. "Who won't make it?"

Maybe a dozen hands went up.

"All right," he said. "We'll start the game with whoever's ready. Looks like Mulridge and McPhee on defense. Hog, Mancini, and Shertzer up front. We've got another full line to hold the fort till the rest of you make it to the bench. I don't want to give the Medicine Hat fans more to cheer about by delaying this game."

Just before I bent to tie my skates, I saw nods from those who would be starting the game with me. They were ready. I knew we could do it.

John Mancini was ready—no surprise—to open the game for his shift as centerman. But then, he was always ready for anything. Skinny, quick, and short-tempered, he caused more brawls than a shipful of rowdy sailors.

The latter characteristic surprised a lot of people, since Mancini had blond hair and the face of an angel.

Louie Shertzer, our big redheaded right winger was just the opposite. You'd think someone with a carrot-top like his would get mad at anything. Nope. Nothing riled this guy, not even when we called him by his nickname, Sumo, because he was built as wide as a Japanese Sumo wrestler.

Hog Burnell, the left winger, was also just finishing the last knots on his skates. This guy's upper body was so big that when he didn't wear shoulder pads under his sweater, you couldn't tell the difference. Plus he was tough. I'd seen him take a puck in the face and just grunt, then score a goal and finally go back to the bench for five stitches.

When our team walked through the tunnel out to ice level, boos and jeers greeted us.

We skated three times around our half of the rink, fired a half-dozen shots on Robbie Patterson, our goalie, and that was it for warm-ups. I didn't even have time to build up my usual pre-game nervousness. Usually I skated in my own world and watched the crowd and worried if I was going to make an idiot of myself in front of those thousands of people. This game, the ref dropped the puck at center before I'd even taken a deep breath.

Mancini fought hard for the puck as the crowd roared. He managed to spin and throw a hip into the opposing center, while at the same time flicking the puck back toward me.

Their winger rushed in.

I stickhandled the puck briefly. With no time to warm-up, I didn't have any feel. So instead of trying a fancy move, I did the safe thing. I fired the puck across to Mulridge, who in turn banked it up the boards to Hog on the left wing. Hog caught the puck in his skates without losing a stride, booted it ahead to his stick, ducked around the defenseman, with Shertzer taking out his winger and Mancini busting in hard from the other side. Just like that, our first play of the game was a two-on-one.

Jason Mulridge and I moved up the ice to follow the play and reached the blue line just as Hog slid the puck across to Mancini. Mancini boomed his slap shot*, and it hit the post in the outside edge. A ringing of metal sounded clearly above the screams of the fans. Their defenseman picked up the rebound and wisely fired it along the boards, trying to zing it past Jason on the blue line.

Jason managed to get a tiny piece of his stick on the puck as it skidded past. Not enough to slow it down. Just enough to tick the puck. Otherwise their defenseman would have been called for icing*.

Since the icing call was waved off, Robbie Patterson left our net to skate into the left corner and wait for the puck. Normally, this was a routine play. It gave Robbie the choice of flicking the puck ahead to our forward, or, if one of the Tiger players moved in too fast, Robbie could spin and fire the puck around the boards and behind the net to me.

Except this time, it wasn't routine. Robbie said later

he was still cold, and he didn't feel quite ready for the game.

In other words, he wasn't too sure of himself. Or of his position on the ice.

When he turned to shoot the puck behind the net, he misjudged his position and missed the angle. He only missed by the length of a hockey stick. But it was enough.

Instead of firing the puck behind the net, he put it into the left corner of his own open net.

The crowd roared laughter and cheered and booed all at the same time.

Less than thirty seconds of playing time had passed, and we were down by a goal to the Tigers, a goal our own goalie had scored against us.

The rest of the game went downhill from there. We were messed up from getting to the rink late and even more messed up by that early goal. We were so messed up that in one game, we made more mistakes than an average team makes in an entire season.

The game was not pretty. Nor was the result. Seven to nothing for the Tigers.

I made sure to avoid the newspaper the next day.

Eight

We had a two-day break until the Prince Albert Raiders visited us in Red Deer. Unfortunately, it did not mean a two-day break from hockey. Coach Blair worked us hard in practice, so hard that Jason's legs cramped on him and the trainer had to drag him off the ice.

At school, Mr. Palmer had a great time in English class, pointing out how embarrassing it is to score on your own net and then to lose by seven goals.

I had no answer, something else he was delighted to point out. I sat in class and vowed to myself that no matter what, we were going to beat the Raiders. We needed to. With sixteen games left in the season, we had to win twelve of them to make the playoffs.

As I drove up to the Centrium arena at four o'clock on game day, I saw Coach Blair and our assistant coach, Thomas Kimball, in the parking lot. They were leaning against Kimball's truck.

"Hello, Coach Blair," I said. "Hello, Mr. Kimball."

They both nodded hello.

"Ready for tonight, B. T.?" Mr. Kimball asked. He was a tall, skinny guy with a tight crew cut. He was around thirty years old. He ran a construction company, and his pickup truck, like now, was always loaded with lumber and other supplies. Since today was a game day, he was wearing a suit and tie, but he always showed up for practices in work boots, jeans, and a T-shirt.

"More than ready," I answered.

"Good."

They waved, and I kept walking.

I would not have given the incident any more thought, except for what happened later that evening during the game against the Raiders. If it hadn't happened to us, it might have been funny.

The game started off fine. In fact, it started off great. Early in the first period, I had the puck along the boards in our end. The Raiders' center lined me up to deck me into the boards, but I saw him out of the corner of my eye and managed to stop. He crashed the boards just in front of me, which brought a big cheer from our home-town crowd. As he staggered to keep his balance, I pushed the puck past him and started to skate around him. He was mad at missing the body check* and swung his stick around, clipping me just behind the knee. I fell. The ref called a tripping penalty, and for the next two minutes of the power play* we had a one-man advantage.

Better yet, I managed to score on the power play. Mancini was in deep behind the Raiders' net. He flipped the puck around the boards, a perfect pass that landed softly on my stick blade. I faked a slap shot, cut in to the center, and fired high and hard. The goalie was screened, and didn't know I had scored until the crowd roared.

It was all we needed to get the crowd into the game. And it makes a difference when the fans are yelling and cheering every time you touch the puck. By the end of the first period, we were ahead by two. By the middle of the second period, we had increased our lead to four goals. Unfortunately, by the end of the second period, disaster began to slowly wash over us.

We made a line change for a faceoff* in the Raiders' end. I stepped onto the ice along with Jason Mulridge and the first string forwards, Mancini, Burnell, and Shertzer.

"Oh man," Hog Burnell moaned as we skated toward the faceoff circle. "I'm going crazy."

"What kind of crazy?"

"Itchy crazy," he said.

My first thought was cockroaches. "Can't be," I said. "I saw you shaking out your equipment."

It was team tradition now. As we pulled each piece of equipment out of our duffel bags, we banged it upside down. We still hadn't figured out how cockroaches got into Jason's equipment, let alone remained hidden and unmoving until just before the ref dropped the puck. As a result, we were more than nervous about it happening again.

"Not cockroaches," Burnell said. "More like a rash."

"Rash?"

We were skating slowly and he looked from side to side to make sure no one could hear him. "Like a diaper rash," he whispered. "It's killing me."

He played the next shift like it actually was killing him. We didn't score or get scored on, but it was not a great shift for any of us. I noticed Mancini squirming as he skated off the ice into the players' box. And I noticed a couple of the other guys grabbing their hockey pants and tugging them from side to side as they skated onto the ice.

By the end of the second period, nearly everyone was groaning. Including me.

I had an itch on the inside of my thighs that felt like ants were trying to chew through my skin. The itch began to spread, going up my stomach and toward my chest.

The Raiders scored three goals on us in the last five minutes of the second period, and none of us cared. All we wanted to do was get to the dressing room and find out what was causing the horrible itching.

"Guys!" Coach Blair yelled as we marched into the dressing room at the end of the second period. "What is going on out there?! Three goals! You had them dead and let them off the hook!"

No one answered. We were all frantically undoing our skates.

"Guys!" Coach Blair shouted.

Skates off, then hockey pants. I rolled down my long johns and looked at the skin on my legs. Then I lifted my T-shirt. No ants. That was the good news. The bad news was that my skin was red and blotchy. And so itchy I wanted a chain saw to cut my legs off and sandpaper to get rid of the skin on my stomach.

Other guys were moaning and pointing at the same thing on their legs.

"Guys!" Coach Blair shouted again. "What is this?"

Players all started complaining at once about an itchy, burning feeling, like a diaper rash.

Coach Blair buried his face in his hands. He stayed that way for a minute. Then he lifted his head. "Teddy," he barked, "it's got to be the laundry. Did you wash everything since practice?"

"Sure did, Coach."

Assistant Coach Kimball looked over at Mancini, who had his T-shirt off. Kimball shook his head in disgust. "I haven't seen a rash like that since I left a sample of fiberglass insulation in my pants pocket—"

Kimball snapped his fingers at a sudden realization. "My wife washed my pants and the fiberglass mixed right into my jeans. I wore them the next day and got the worst rash I'd ever had."

"Teddy," Coach Blair snapped. "Check the washing machine and the filter on the dryer."

Teddy had his own room just down the hall where he did all the laundry and repaired rips in socks and sweaters. Without a word, Teddy jogged out of the dressing room.

Minutes later he returned, holding a soggy lump of pink goo.

"Fiberglass," he said. "Someone played a nasty trick, all right. They must have thrown this in while the washing machine was going."

We scrambled to get out of our gear. Most of us wore long johns beneath our equipment to absorb the sweat. We replaced what we could with the clothing we had worn to the game. It helped, but only a little.

We played like a crippled team in the third period. With one minute left in the game, the Raiders scored to tie.

I remembered how mad I had been in English class when Mr. Palmer taunted me about the team's losing streak. No one would understand why we gave up this four-goal lead, because itchy long johns was probably an excuse we would keep to ourselves.

"Jason," I said as we skated onto the ice for the last shift of the game. "I don't care what it takes. Get me the puck."

He grinned. "It's yours pal."

He kept his promise.

Mancini lost the faceoff, and the puck squirted ahead to the Raiders' winger. The winger moved toward Jason, and Jason bumped him into the boards, found the puck, and fired it across the ice to me.

I only had eyes for the Raiders' net. I broke past their other winger, and had full speed as I reached the Raiders' blue line. Mancini and Shertzer broke wide as we crossed into their end. One of their defensemen drifted over to cover them. It left me alone with only one guy to beat. I ducked my head like I was going to cut inside, pushed one step outside, then moved back in toward the center.

The double fake worked. It gave me a split-second opening, and I took advantage of it by pounding a slap shot. It dinged the post, kicked straight out toward Shertzer. The goalie tried to spin himself in Shertzer's direction but didn't have time. Shertzer banged the puck into the wide open side of the net.

Bingo!

The crowd erupted like a volcano, and we skated off the ice with a victory. The way we danced around and celebrated in the dressing room made it look like we'd won the Stanley Cup, not just broken a losing streak.

My joy didn't last long though. When I walked out to the parking lot, I passed Assistant Coach Kimball's construction company truck. It was loaded with lumber. And with rolls of mesh wire. And with one other thing I hadn't noticed earlier.

Fiberglass insulation.

 *Nine*

Very few of the players on the Red Deer Rebels actually came from Red Deer. Our hometowns were other places, mainly across the western Canadian provinces. During the season we stayed with Red Deer families who took us in.

These families are called billets. The Rebels pay them for our rent and groceries, but billets don't expect to make money off us. As hockey players, we eat a lot.

Instead, billet families usually love hockey and want to help out. They do their best to make us feel at home. My own billets, the Henrys, were no different.

That's why I was surprised when lunch was quiet the day after we beat the Prince Albert Raiders.

There were just the three of us sitting in the sunlight of their dining room: me, Mr. Henry, and his wife.

The dining room was my favorite room in the house. The Henrys lived in the part of Red Deer known as Sunnybrook, and their house was on the edge of a park.

The dining room had large glass patio doors, and it overlooked trees on a steep hill that led down to a small creek. Some mornings, when I got up early and sat there in the quiet, I would see deer wander up to the fence of the backyard.

I was into my second tuna sandwich and neither Mr. Henry nor his wife had asked me a single question about the game.

I took my eyes away from the trees and blue sky and looked over at them.

They were staring at me. Not eating. Just staring.

I looked behind me to see if a couple of deer had appeared or if a blue jay had landed on the bird feeder just outside the patio doors. Maybe that had their attention.

Nope. Nothing behind me.

I looked back at them. They were still staring in my direction. Still saying nothing.

"Excuse me," I said.

They nodded.

I went to the bathroom to see if I was growing a huge purple pimple somewhere on my face that I had not noticed yet.

The mirror showed me a face that looked identical to the photo in the team program. Brownish hair. Brown eyes. An okay-looking face. Not much of a smile. Fortunately, no monster pimple. So they couldn't have been staring at that.

I walked back to the dining room and took my chair at the table.

They looked at me.

I coughed.

They said nothing.

"Um, we won last night," I said.

"I know," Mr. Henry said. "We were there."

Strange he hadn't said anything about the game-winning goal.

"Still lots to go," I said. "We still have to win eleven out of the last fifteen games to make the playoffs."

"I know," Mr. Henry said. He was a thin man with round glasses who usually wore a brown sweater of some kind. He removed his glasses and polished them with a napkin.

It was definitely strange that he said nothing else. Usually he had tons of questions: He wanted to know if the referees did a good job, wanted to know what I thought of our chances to make the playoffs.

Now, nothing.

Mrs. Henry was nicely plump in her expensive sweat suit, the kind of plump mother you'd want if you needed a mother to hold you when you were sad. Which I definitely did not ever need or want, but I could see how she'd be nice for someone who did.

She finally broke the silence. "We didn't know you had a girlfriend."

I swallowed a big chunk of tuna sandwich. "Neither did I," I said. "You know I'm concentrating on hockey."

"Sure," Mr. Henry said. He didn't look like he believed me.

I'm no psychic, but I can tell when something is wrong. I set my sandwich down on my plate.

"What exactly is going on?" I asked.

Mrs. Henry looked at her husband. She twisted her fingers together. "Tell him," she said.

Mr. Henry cleared his throat. He stared down at the table as he spoke. "We got a phone call this morning from a very angry father."

I didn't understand where this was going.

"Yes?" I said.

"He told us if you ever beat up his daughter again on a date, he would send the police over."

"What?" I said. It didn't sound like Mr. Henry was joking.

"We can help you," Mrs. Henry said. "We know some very good counselors. Perhaps if you talk to someone . . ."

"Look," I said. I spoke very slowly because I was getting very angry. "I don't have a girlfriend. I don't beat people up."

"Please," Mr. Henry said, "don't make this more difficult than it already is. We're worried you might get into some serious legal trouble. And if the newspapers get hold of this story . . ."

"You don't believe me," I said. "I have no idea why anyone would call and tell you those lies, but you're going to believe a stranger over me aren't you?"

"Brian Thomas," Mrs. Henry began in her soft voice.

"Yes?" I felt very cold inside, and my voice probably showed it.

"You're a very quiet young man," she said. "You'll talk to us about hockey when we ask, but you never say anything about yourself. You go for those long drives at night. So after the phone call, we tried to reach your mother and—"

I stood. "You what?"

"We tried to call your mother. Mr. Henry and I talked it over, and we thought it would be the best thing to—"

"I don't have a mother," I said. My voice was so low that they had to lean forward to hear. "I stopped having a mother the day she walked out on me and my dad. Understand?"

"Brian—"

Standing in front of them, I slammed my fist down on the table. "I do not have a girlfriend. I did not beat anyone up."

Mr. Henry stood to face me. He was shorter, and I could see the top of his hair where it got thin.

"Brian," he said. "We worry about you. You're so quiet. You don't have many friends here. We just want to make sure—"

"I don't need friends. I've got hockey."

"And you're very good," he said quickly, "one of the most promising juniors anyone has seen in quite some time. But you have to develop a life outside of hockey. What will happen if for some reason you couldn't play hockey? Then what?"

I looked him straight in the eye. "For some reason, like if I got thrown in jail for beating up a girl?"

He gulped. His adam's apple bobbed up and down above his brown sweater.

"I'm only saying this one more time," I said. "No

girlfriend. No fight. If you don't believe me, I'll pack my bags today."

I hit them with logic. "If the guy was telling the truth, why didn't he tell you his name? Or his daughter's name?"

Mr. Henry frowned as he thought that through. Finally, he let out a big breath. He reached down with one hand and rested it on his wife's shoulder. After far too long, he said, "We believe you. I'll do my best to find out who called here this morning."

I walked out without saying a word. I didn't trust myself or what I might say.

In another two hours practice would begin. That would take my mind off all this. Just me, my skates, a hockey stick, and the ice rink in front of me. My escape.

Ten

Practice did not become much of an escape from my worries. First of all, Coach Blair was still mad at us for losing in Medicine Hat, in spite of our recent win, and worked us hard. Frankie Smith, a fifteen-year-old rookie, threw up over the boards and onto the rubber mat of the players' box.

Second, my equipment didn't feel right. I couldn't figure out exactly why it felt wrong, but I couldn't get comfortable as I skated.

And third, no matter how hard I tried to think about the puck and skating, I couldn't get my mind off what had happened at lunch.

It hurt that the Henrys believed I was the kind of guy who would lie. It hurt that the Henrys believed I was the kind of guy who would beat up a girl. It hurt that the Henrys had tried to phone the woman who only now wanted to say she was my mother because it looked like I might someday get a big, fat contract to play in the National Hockey League.

Not only was I feeling hurt, but it also bothered me that I would actually let my feelings get hurt. Ever since Dad died, I had pushed feelings away. If you didn't have feelings, you couldn't get hurt. Only now it seemed I hadn't done as good a job as I needed.

And on top of all of this, there was the telephone call itself. Who would call the Henrys and tell them I had beat up his daughter? And why?

What if that same person called Coach Blair? Or the newspapers?

I knew I hadn't beaten up anyone. *I* knew I could never beat up a girl. *I* knew I wasn't dating anyone because I wanted to concentrate on hockey. Hockey, unlike girls, could never hurt your feelings.

But no matter how much *I* knew I hadn't done anything, it might not make a difference if someone started spreading the lies. I'd seen enough to know that just the rumors could cause me some major trouble.

"McPhee!" I heard Coach Blair yelling at me. I pulled myself away from my thoughts and looked across the ice at him in the gray and black sweats of the Rebel colors. "You want to skate? Or do you want to push a baby carriage? Get your legs in gear!"

I pushed ahead. The clock showed another fifteen minutes of practice. It seemed like we had been on the ice since before hockey had been invented.

Coach Blair ended practice without giving us any shooting or passing drills. Instead, he kept skating us, blowing the whistle to make us stop, blowing it to make us start, blowing it to make us reverse directions, blowing it to make us very, very sorry for losing so many games.

Finally, the torture ended, and the guys headed back toward our dressing room.

Coach Blair waved me over to him.

The players left the ice. It was just Coach Blair and me and the rows and rows of empty stands that climbed high into the arena around us. And the guy on the Zamboni tractor, ready to clean and water the ice surface.

"McPhee," Coach Blair said. His whistle hung from his neck, quiet for the first time in the last two hours.

"Yes, sir?"

"How are you feeling?"

"Fine." I tried to keep the worry out of my voice. Had someone already called him with the lie about me beating up a girl?

"Good," he said. "The team needs you."

"I'll do my best," I said.

"Could you go a little further than that?" he asked.

"My best is my best," I said. I wasn't trying to be rude. "I always work as hard as I can."

"I don't mean that," he told me. He looked me straight in the eyes. "I mean can you go a little further off the ice?"

"I don't understand."

"With fifteen games left, we need to win eleven more. You know that. I also think you know we can do it. Except for the final two games of the season against Lethbridge, we play some easy teams."

I nodded.

He kept going, still looking me in the eyes. "Don't get me wrong," he said. "I like you. You're a good kid. But I think you should try to get more involved with the team off the ice. You're a natural leader, if you want to be."

"Me?"

"You. Loosen up a bit. Don't make such an effort to be a loner. The guys on this team look up to you. They'd like it if you'd let them become friends. And it would sure help us as a team. I think if we make the playoffs, we'd have as good a chance as anyone at going all the way."

All I could do was nod. It hadn't occurred to me that the guys would like to be my friends. Maybe if I just tried a little.

"That's all," Coach Blair finished. "See what you can do about bringing the guys together in our final stretch of games. All right?"

I nodded again.

"Good. See you in the dressing room."

He skated to get his clipboard where he'd left it on top of one of the nets.

The Zamboni tractor rolled onto the ice.

I skated off and went straight to the dressing room, walking along the long rubber mat that protected our skate blades from the concrete.

When I got to the dressing room, I looked around as if I'd never been in it before, proud of what Coach Blair had said about some of these guys looking up to me. It almost took away some of the bad feelings I had from lunch.

As I looked around, I realized that the guys really were looking up at me. All of them. They were sitting on the benches, staring at me, not saying a word.

"It's all right, guys. I'm still on the team," I joked. "Coach Blair didn't yell too much."

My first joke in two months didn't bring much laughter. The guys kept staring at me.

51

"McPhee," Jason said from where he was sitting, half-undressed, skates unlaced but not yet taken off his feet.

"Yeah?"

"Check your duffel bag," he said. "I think there was a mix-up. You might have my bag."

"No problem," I said. "I'll check."

The dressing room was very, very quiet as I went to my stall. I pulled a duffel bag from my locker. The white number three on the side of the bag was plain against its black nylon.

"Nope," I said. "This is mine."

"Look closer," Jason said. "Mine used to have two threes on it. But last week one of them fell off and I didn't get it fixed yet."

I looked closer. Then I understood. There were the faint outlines of another three where it had peeled away from the black nylon. Jason's number 33 had become a 3.

"You've got my bag?" I asked.

Jason held up the duffel bag at his stall, showing my number 3 on it.

"Nuts," I said, "that explains why my equipment felt weird. We must have gotten them mixed up when we took them off the bus last night."

If there had been a mix-up in skates, we would have noticed it right away, because your skates fit the way they've broken into your feet. Put on someone else's skates, and you know it right away. But one of the things Teddy always did in the morning before practice was pull out our sweaters to clean them, and take our skates to sharpen them. Teddy, of course, would have taken Jason's skates from the duffel bag in my stall and my skates from the duffel bag in Jason's stall, then returned our skates to the right places. Since I'd put on my skates, I had assumed it was my equipment too.

I turned to Jason. "So you wore my equipment and I wore yours," I said. "I'm glad today wasn't the day you had cockroaches."

Again, no one laughed.

Coach Blair walked into the dressing room. He frowned, as he couldn't understand the strange tension in the dressing room.

"Guys?" he asked.

Nobody replied. I was the only one standing. The rest of them still sat.

"McPhee?" Coach Blair asked.

I shrugged. I had no idea what was happening.

Hog Burnell broke the silence.

"Coach," Hog said, "remember when I lost my wallet last week?"

Coach Blair suddenly became suspicious. "Yes, I remember."

"And remember how you told me not to tell anyone? To keep my eyes opened in case it showed up?"

"I remember that too," Coach Blair said. "We weren't going to accuse anyone here of stealing it. Not without good reason. What are you trying to say, Hog?"

Hog pointed at Jason and let him reply.

"Coach," Jason said. "I found it in this duffel bag. I thought it was my duffel bag, and when I went into the side pocket to find my comb, I found Hog's wallet."

"Oh," Coach said. He asked the question he didn't

want to ask. He asked the question I didn't want to hear. "Who's duffel bag?"

"McPhee's," Jason said.

Coach looked at me and gave a grin. It wasn't much of a grin. "I'm sure there's a good explanation," Coach said.

I tried to think of a good explanation. But I didn't have time.

Louie Shertzer spoke. His voice was angry. "Coach, you didn't tell me Hog's wallet had been stolen too."

Coach Blair sighed. He hadn't taken his eyes off me, and he still didn't as he answered Shertzer. "No, I didn't Louie. I didn't want the team knowing that someone had been stealing."

"My wallet too!" Mancini said. "I had fifty bucks in it. Remember, Coach?"

Coach finally turned his head away from me and looked back at Jason. "Did you find anything else in McPhee's duffel bag?"

"Shertzer's wallet," Jason said. "*And* Mancini's. None of the wallets had any money left."

"Guys, it wasn't me," I said. I felt like throwing up at the way they were all looking at me. "I swear it wasn't me. I didn't—"

Coach Blair cut me off. "McPhee, we need to talk. Now."

Nobody said a word as I followed Coach Blair out of the dressing room.

I didn't feel like much of a team leader. And I doubted I had done much to bring the guys together for our final stretch of games.

Eleven

Coach Blair, I didn't steal those wallets," I said, not even waiting until I was completely inside his office.

He shut the door behind me. He moved to his desk and sat in the chair behind it, still wearing his hockey skates.

"It looks bad, McPhee. Real bad."

"I did not put those wallets there." I was too scared to be mad. My words felt like a waterfall of marbles dropping from my mouth. "Someone else must have. I would never steal from—"

"You're not listening," he said. "It *looks* bad. Whether you stole those wallets or not, we've got a real problem."

"Coach?"

He rubbed his face with both hands. While I waited for him to speak, I stared at a photo on the edge of his desk of his pretty blond wife with their baby boy.

"McPhee," he finally said, "I really want to believe you."

He watched my face. He probably saw I was thinking he *wanted* to believe me. Not he *did* believe me.

"I'm sorry," he said seconds later. "What I meant is I do believe you. Someone else put those wallets there."

He had apologized too late, though. It hurt. The Henrys. Coach. Did I keep to myself so much that no one felt they knew me enough to trust me?

"Someone else did," I insisted. I was starting to be less scared now and more mad. *Who was trying to get me? And why?*

"Don't you see?" Coach Blair said. "Unless we prove who did it . . ."

"It looks like I'm guilty," I finished.

"Hockey's a team game," he said. "Can we be a team if the rest of the guys think you stole from them?"

I couldn't answer. Not because I didn't know the answer, but because I couldn't get the words out.

We stared at each other.

"You'll have to sit out a few games," he said. "I hate to do it. The team needs your skills on defense."

Miss some games? I felt like a miserable wall of bricks standing there in my hockey equipment, sweat running down my face, my stick in my hand.

"How many games?" I asked.

"I don't know," he said. "Until we find out who did this."

I got the feeling he didn't expect to find anyone else. I got the feeling he did think I had stolen the wallets but found it easier to pretend someone else had.

"There was fiberglass in Mr. Kimball's truck," I said. "And—"

"Stop!" Coach Blair said. He was angry. "I'm not stupid. I saw the insulation there too. But don't even try to accuse him. Think about it McPhee. Anyone else could have done it. Maybe taken it from his truck. Or gotten their own fiberglass, knowing he's in construction and how it would make him look bad. A lot of other people had access to the washing machine. Even the stickboys, for crying out loud. And don't think I'm not looking into all of this."

"Yes, sir," I said. "I'm sorry. Maybe . . ." I started to tell him about the phone call to the Henrys, then I stopped. Maybe Coach Blair wouldn't think someone was out to get me. Maybe instead Coach Blair would think that a person who would steal wallets from his teammates would also beat up a girl on a date.

"Yes?" he asked.

"Nothing," I said.

He stood. "Maybe you should wait in here while the guys finish showering."

"Sure." For the first time in a long time, I was close to tears. It was sinking in. I was now shut out from my own team.

"I'll issue a news release that says you went home for urgent personal reasons," Coach Blair said. "It won't be a lie, because it might be best if you weren't in town while this gets sorted out."

"Sure," I said.

"I hope we can keep this a team secret," Coach Blair said. "If this gets out, there won't be many teams in this league who will want you to play for them."

Twelve

Red Deer to my hometown of Winnipeg is about a fourteen-hour drive if you don't hit any blizzards and you don't take any breaks and you only stop to fill up on gas. It might be a few hours less for someone who has a faster vehicle than my 1972 pickup truck, but it's definitely fourteen hours for me. I know. I drove to Red Deer from Winnipeg just after Christmas when I was traded from the Brandon Wheat Kings.

Only this time as I drove, I wasn't quite so happy. This time, I wasn't driving somewhere to play hockey. I was driving because I might never play hockey again.

And it was not a great place to be driving when my head was filled with such depressing thoughts. I was in the darkness at nine o'clock at night, on a deserted two-lane prairie highway somewhere between Hannah, Alberta, and Kindersly, Saskatchewan. The wind blew hard against my windshield, rocking the truck as it groaned along the highway. The noise of the wind as it came through the cracks of my windows was like the wailing of a sad song, and it didn't help my mood at all.

Never play hockey again?

If the newspapers got hold of why I was driving to Winnipeg, no other team in the league would take me. Without junior hockey, I would never make the NHL.

It wasn't as if I had lots to make my life happy. I was on my way to the home that wasn't really my home in Winnipeg. My dad had died when I was twelve. A brain tumor. He had found out one month, and the next month he was gone. My mom had already left by then, so I ended up with my aunt and uncle. They didn't really mind having me there. But they didn't go out of their way to treat me like their own kid either. Mostly, I just felt invisible.

Except when I was on the ice. Then, even though I was always scared of making a mistake, I felt like I belonged someplace.

Never play hockey again? My whole life was hockey. What else could there be for me if I couldn't play hockey or dream about hockey?

With the wind blowing through my old truck, I couldn't seem to stay warm. I turned up the heater and shivered and bounced behind the steering wheel as my worn-out tires hummed down the highway. In the last ten minutes, I had not seen the headlights of a single car or truck.

I had never felt so alone.

So I did something I had told myself I would not do as I drove. I turned on the radio to listen to the Red Deer

Rebels as they played the Regina Pats back in the Centrium.

I cranked the volume to hear above the wind and highway noises of my old truck.

I was just in time for a commercial. I listened to a singing cow tell me why I should drink milk as much as possible. Finally the game returned.

"Five minutes and thirty seconds left in a very exciting game," the announcer said. "Red Deer Rebels with five goals. The Regina Pats with five goals. Faceoff in the Rebel zone."

I stared straight ahead into the yellow beams of my headlights. I should have been playing this game.

"Puck dropped back to the Regina defense. He takes his stick back. And—"

The announcer's voice rose with excitement. "A booooomer of a slap shot. A direct shot on net! The goalie makes the save. . . . No! Folks, that puck went into the net! It's a goal! Six-to-five for the Regina Pats."

It figured. All I had to do was turn the radio on for the Rebels to start losing the game.

"It was the strangest thing folks," the announcer was saying. "From up here it looked like Robbie Patterson in the Rebels' net had managed to get his glove out in time to catch the booming slap shot. Then somehow the puck dribbled past him anyway. And folks . . .

"What's this? Here comes Patterson skating out of the net toward the players' bench. He appears to be holding his glove out. He's shaking it and pointing at it. I can't quite see what is . . .

"Folks. He's right at the bench. Coach Blair is taking a close look at the glove and . . .

"Folks, Rebel time-out. Coach Blair has called a time-out."

What was going on? Patterson never got upset like this.

The radio cut back to the singing cow. Then to five reasons I should switch brands of baby diapers. I definitely preferred being on the ice over listening to the game on the radio.

"We're back, folks," the announcer said. "In all my years of hockey, I've never seen a slap shot so hard it actually snapped the webbing of a goalie glove! Robbie Patterson had made the save, and the puck just kept right on going. What a bad break for the Rebels. B. T. McPhee, their star defenseman out for an indefinite length of time. Now this. What's it going to take for the Rebels to make the playoffs? If the Rebels keep this bad streak going, and if it's true the Rebels are for sale, you can figure the team will be worth a lot less by the time this season ends. What can the coach and general manager be thinking about this latest bad break, I wonder. . . ."

The announcer took a breath. He'd done his job of filling air time until the ref was ready to drop the puck again.

"Here they are folks. About to start the game with just over five minutes left. Rebels down by a goal. Mancini at center ice, fights for the puck, knocks it ahead. Hog Burnell skating in—"

I snapped the radio off. I couldn't take listening when I should have been playing. Mancini, Hog, Shertzer. I missed them. And they didn't miss me.

I banged the steering wheel with the palm of my hand. Hours and hours of driving ahead of me. It was going to be the worst trip of my life, sitting in this old truck and with nothing but these depressing thoughts for company.

Bad breaks the announcer had said? No kidding. It was like someone was doing their best to make sure we lost.

It hit me as my last thought sunk in.

Someone was doing their best to make sure we lost.

I added it up. Cockroaches in Jason's equipment. My skate rivets loosened. Cola dumped in the players' bench. Flat tires. Fiberglass in the laundry. A wrecked goalie's glove.

Maybe it wasn't that someone was trying to wreck *my* life with the skate rivets and the phone call to the Henrys and the stolen wallets in my duffel bag. Maybe those were just more ways to try to hurt the team.

As the wind noise died down, I realized I had taken my foot off the gas pedal and had let the truck slow down.

If someone really was trying to make the Rebels lose, I had to find out. Because if I could find out, we still might make the playoffs. And I might be able to play hockey again.

I hit the brakes and swung the truck back toward Red Deer.

 **Thirteen**

A little over an hour later, I was halfway back to Red Deer. I passed a service station just as dark and lonely as the highway. The only light shone in the parking lot over a telephone booth.

Just down the highway from the service station, an idea hit me. I told myself it was a dumb idea. But I couldn't get it out of my head. And I kept thinking about the telephone booth in the parking lot.

I turned the truck around and spent a few minutes driving back to the closed service station.

I parked my truck beside the telephone booth. Again I tried to tell myself how stupid my idea was. Except I couldn't think of another way. If I could figure out what questions to ask, who else in Red Deer might help me?

I got out of the truck, still telling myself it was a stupid idea.

I also half hoped the telephone book would be missing. But there it was, dangling from a steel cable.

I sighed.

I half hoped there would be a whole bunch of Holbrooks in the book, because that would give me the perfect excuse to quit even before I started. Unfortunately, there was only one Holbrook listed in the Red Deer section of the telephone directory. A Frederick Holbrook. On 53rd Street.

I sighed again. I dialed the number before I could change my mind.

A voice came on the line and told me to deposit seventy-five cents. I thanked the voice before I realized it was a recording. I wasn't sure if this was a good start to making a phone call at ten at night to a girl I had hardly ever spoken to.

I pushed three quarters into the coin slot and listened to the phone ring.

I half hoped no one would answer. Unfortunately, it only rang twice before a quiet voice said hello.

"Hello," I said back, trying to sound mature. "May I speak with Cheryl Holbrook."

"This is Cheryl."

Great. What do I say next?

I must have waited too long.

"This is Cheryl," she said again.

I couldn't do it.

"I'm sorry," I said. "I must have dialed the wrong number. Good-bye."

"Wait!" She laughed. "How could you have dialed the wrong number if you asked for me?"

I wanted to hit my head against the wall of the phone booth. So much for being a guy who always used logic.

All it took was a girl's soft voice and my mind turned to mush. I tried to think of something fast.

"I got the wrong Cheryl Holbrook," I finally said. "So sorry. Good-bye."

"Wait!" She laughed again. "How do you know it's the wrong Cheryl Holbrook?"

This was much harder than facing 200-pound forwards who wanted to smear me into the boards. I again did my best to find an excuse.

"Are you old and fat and wrinkled?" I asked.

"Um, no," she said.

"That's it then. Wrong Cheryl Holbrook," I told her. "The one I'm looking for is old and fat and wrinkled. I guess I should be going now."

"Is this Brian McPhee?" she asked.

I wanted to crawl under my truck. I should have hung up, but I was too rattled. I clutched the phone and gulped a few dozen times, trying to get some air. No wonder I stayed away from women and concentrated on hockey.

"Is it?" she asked again. "Is this Brian?"

I mumbled it was.

"I thought I recognized your voice from English class. How nice you called."

"Um, thanks," I said. I wondered what to say next.

"Well," she said after a few seconds of silence, "did you get your homework done for Mr. Palmer's class tomorrow?"

Hadn't she heard that I was leaving town for urgent personal reasons? Hadn't she heard what Coach Blair had told the newspapers and radio?

"I didn't," I said. "It might not be that important if—"

A voice interrupted and told me to put in another fifty cents for two more minutes.

I reached into my pockets. Nothing.

"Hang on!" I shouted into the phone.

I dropped the phone and raced back to the truck. In the ashtray I usually had some change. I found three gum wrappers, five pennies, and one quarter. I rammed my hand into the seat cushions. Sometimes money falls from my pocket when I drive. I ripped a fingernail on a spring in the cushion but managed to find another quarter. I raced back to the phone and plugged the money into the slot.

"Brian? Brian?" she was asking. "Are you trying to be funny?"

"No!" I said. I sucked in some air.

"It has been a strange phone call," she told me.

"I don't always think too well when I'm in trouble," I said.

"Trouble?" Her voice instantly sounded worried. To my surprise, I found I liked that.

"Not big, big trouble." *No,* I told myself, *only trouble that might mean the end of my hockey career.* "Could you meet me tomorrow morning before school starts?"

"Sure," she said. "At the main doors of the school?"

"No!" I took a breath. "I mean, would it be okay if we met somewhere else?"

The last thing I wanted was to risk running into one of the guys on the team.

"Where?" she asked.

I thought of one of the main streets in Red Deer.

"Maybe a restaurant. Do you know the one on Ross Street down by city hall park?"

She waited a few seconds. I hoped the phone wouldn't run out of time. I didn't think I had any change left in the cushions of the truck.

"Sure," she said. "Quarter after eight?"

"That would be great." I found myself grinning into the darkness of the phone booth. "Thanks."

She said good-bye and hung up.

I continued to drive back toward Red Deer and stopped in Innisfail, a small town just south of Red Deer. I found a motel there and spent a lonely night staring at the ceiling in the rented room. It didn't help that I heard on the late news that the Rebels had lost again. We needed to win eleven games, and we only had fourteen games to do it.

Fourteen

Why did you call me for help?" she asked.

We sat in the restaurant by the park. It was only half-full. Our waitress dropped off our toast and coffee and then decided to ignore us.

I took a sip of my coffee. The stuff tasted awful. I tried not to make a face because I wanted the coffee to make me look more mature.

"Good question," I said as I looked across the table at her. Cheryl Holbrook was definitely not old and fat and wrinkled. I had known that from the first time I saw her in class. But in class I'd always been afraid of getting caught staring at her.

Now, in the restaurant by the park, I had every excuse to look. Her eyes were light green, which was a nice contrast to her blond hair. Her nose had a few light freckles, and her cheeks had little dimples when she smiled.

However, she soon stopped smiling at me. She leaned

forward, her elbows on the table, and she watched me with a serious half-frown.

"Come on," she said. "If it's a good question, answer it. Why me?"

"Why you? Easy."

Only it wasn't easy. How could I explain that I didn't have any friends in Red Deer? How could I explain that I hoped she would remember how I had argued with Mr. Palmer for her when I first got to the school?

"Easy," I repeated. "It's . . . um . . . because . . ."

"You think I'm a sucker for a pretty face," she said.

I felt myself blush. I knew I didn't have a pretty face.

She laughed. "Don't sweat it. Why not tell me about your trouble and how I can help?"

I nodded and sipped more coffee. The taste hadn't changed at all. I dumped three spoons of sugar and some cream into it.

"My trouble is that someone has been doing things to make hockey real tough for me," I said.

Her eyebrows lifted. "During the games?"

"During and after and before."

"Oh," she said. I noticed she wasn't drinking her coffee. "How tough has it been?"

"You probably know I didn't play last night," I answered.

She shook her head. "No," she said. "Please don't take it personally, but I don't follow hockey."

I thought about that for a second. "Actually, I think I like that. Some girls chase anybody who plays junior hockey. At least if you help me, I'll know it won't be for that reason."

Tiny circles of red appeared on her cheeks, and she quickly looked down at her coffee. She added some sugar to it.

"What kind of trouble?" she asked without looking up.

I took a breath. This was the hard part. I either trusted her completely and told her everything or I didn't ask for her help at all.

I told her everything. The cockroaches, the skate rivets, the fiberglass in our long johns, the snapped glove, the phone call to the Henrys, and how I had been blamed for stealing the wallets.

She watched me as I spoke. She listened carefully until I was finished.

"You are innocent." She said it like a statement, not like a question.

"I didn't take the wallets. I don't even have a girlfriend."

For some reason, those tiny circles of red showed on her cheeks again, and she went back to looking at her coffee.

"How do you think I can help?" she asked. "I don't know anything about hockey." She stirred her coffee.

"I have two problems," I said. "One is that I don't know where to begin asking questions to find out who's behind this. Two, even if I knew the questions, I couldn't ask them. I'm supposed to be in Winnipeg."

Cheryl took a notebook from the backpack she had dropped onto the chair beside her. She set the notebook on the table and got a pen ready.

"Repeat everything you told me," she said.

I did. She made notes. Then for about five minutes, she carefully studied what she had written.

The waitress stopped by to pour more coffee into our cups. It made me grumpy because that meant I'd have to start over trying to finish the horrible stuff.

Cheryl flipped to a different page of her notebook and began writing again.

I poured more sugar and cream into my coffee and stirred.

"All right," Cheryl finally said. She ripped the page out of her notebook. "You need to answer these questions for me."

She read them out. "First, why would someone want you off the team? If you can't answer that, then try to figure out how someone would gain if you were off the team."

"Gain?"

"Whoever is doing it must have a reason. How will it help this person if you are gone?"

"I don't know," I said. "Maybe—"

"I want you to think about these questions all day. I want the answers down as a report."

"Sure—"

She held up a hand to interrupt me again. "Plus, I'd like a list of all the people who are able to get into the players' dressing room whenever they want. Someone might be able to sneak in once, maybe twice, but any more often is taking a big chance of getting caught. I'd say whoever is doing this is usually allowed in there."

"They'd only have to get in twice," I argued. "Once to

put the cockroaches in Jason's duffel bag and once to get at my skates."

"The wallets," she reminded me. "Three different wallets stolen at three different times. Plus the time those wallets were put into your duffel bag. And what about the goalie's glove?"

I whistled in admiration. "Impressive. Why do I feel a lot better all of a sudden?"

"Just get the answers ready for me."

"Should I call you at home later?"

She stared over my shoulder and tapped her front teeth as she thought. "No," she said, "meet me here tonight around eight o'clock. Can you do that?"

"How about earlier?" I asked. Waiting around all day would kill me. "Maybe we could meet after school?"

"No, I have some of my own questions to answer." She didn't tell me more.

"Tonight at eight then." I took a mouthful of coffee and swallowed. It was worse than medicine.

I watched Cheryl stir her coffee. She had long pretty fingers. As her spoon clanked against the cup, I realized it was still full. She hadn't taken one sip of coffee—she just kept stirring it! I laughed.

She lifted her head quickly. Surprised.

"You laughed," she said.

I thought about it. "Yes, I guess I did."

"*And* you smiled. I didn't know you could do those things."

I tried another smile. It didn't feel too bad.

"So, what was so funny?" she asked.

I grinned. "I hate coffee too."

Fifteen

I didn't have to go far from the restaurant to find a place to spend the rest of the day. I crossed Ross Street, walked across city hall park, and entered the library, a white, square two-story building.

On the second floor, I found a chair at a window that overlooked the park. For the first hour, I mainly stared at the park with its dead, brown grass and piles of snow left to melt. In the summer, I thought, this would be a nice view, with green grass and the trees filled with leaves and the dirt beds blooming with flowers. But summer seemed so far away. I wondered if I would still be a hockey player then or if my hopes and dreams of playing in the NHL would be over.

It seemed stupid to think that answering the questions on Cheryl's note paper might get me back on the team. I let myself become depressed, until I told myself it was the only chance I had. So for the next couple of hours I concentrated hard on answering the questions as best I could.

I also made a list of people I thought could have hurt the team and the reasons why I suspected them. I underlined Assistant Coach Kimball. If he had done these things, it was very smart of him to be the one to first mention fiberglass as a possibility. Like being a thief and being the one to first discover a theft. No one would suspect you. But I suspected him anyway. Of course, there were the stickboys, but why would they do this stuff? Or for that matter why would Kimball? I got a big headache trying to figure out who was doing this to our team.

After that, I still had too much time to kill.

I decided to stay in the library. It wasn't likely that many of the Rebels players would hang out at the library. I would be safe here.

I read for the rest of the day.

"Hey!" Cheryl said when she stepped up to my table in the restaurant at eight o'clock sharp. "How are you doing?"

"Great," I lied. I wasn't hopeful this would help. Still, I did feel better just to see her smile.

"Me too," she said as she sat opposite me. "I'm glad for the chance to help you out, but I'm also discovering this detective work is plain fun. Count me in for as long as this takes."

The waitress came by and we both ordered milkshakes. Not coffee.

"Fire away," Cheryl said, still grinning. "What did you come up with?"

I unfolded the sheet of paper and read my messy writing. "I don't know why someone would want me off the team," I said. "I don't have any enemies—or at least I didn't until the wallet incident."

"Who will gain if you're gone?"

"Cheryl, I spent a lot of time thinking about this. I suppose a couple of the second or third line defensemen might gain."

"What do you mean?"

"With me gone, they'll get extra ice time. A chance to play more." I scratched my head. "But that won't help them much if we don't make the playoffs."

Cheryl grinned. "And with you off the team, the Rebels probably *won't* make the playoffs."

"I'm not trying to say that . . ."

"Why not?" she said. "I asked my dad about you. He said you were brought to the team just to help them win. He said you are one of the best defensemen in the league. He said since you joined the team, it has won eighty percent of its home games and sixty-five percent of away games. He said—"

"Come on," I said. My face was growing hot. I was happy the waitress stopped by at that moment with our milkshakes. Slurping on the straw gave me something to do besides squirm and stare at my fingernails.

Cheryl drank some of her milkshake, then spoke. "So maybe the question should be who will gain if the team doesn't make the playoffs?"

"No one," I said. "The guys on the team won't. Coach Blair won't—he might lose his job. Shoot, the Rebels might even get sold and moved to another town. The owners want us to make the playoffs so they can have good ticket sales."

"Right." Cheryl was grinning, like I'd proved her point. But I didn't know what point it was.

"Right?"

"Do you know what my dad does?" she asked.

I shook my head no.

"He's an insurance investigator, which means he checks out insurance claims. A lot of times people try different scams to rip off insurance companies. His job is to look for the scams. He's almost like a detective."

"A good person to go to with questions," I said.

She agreed. "I asked Dad who would gain if the Rebels didn't make the playoffs, and he said everything you did."

"And?"

"And he also went one step further. The less money the Rebels make as a team, the less expensive they would be to buy."

I set my milkshake down so suddenly it clanked on the table. "That's who would gain! The person buying the team!"

"Yes." She was still grinning. "I asked my dad these questions at lunch today. He said he would help out. And he did."

She pulled a file from her knapsack and shoved it across the table at me. "Dad has a lot of business connections here in Red Deer. It didn't take him long to find out who was trying to buy the team."

I opened the folder. It had articles from various magazines. The first article showed a bald man. He was dressed in a pin-striped suit and sitting behind a huge desk, smoking a cigar, and smiling into the camera. One of his front teeth was shiny gold.

"Jonathan Sullivan," I read from the headline. "Real estate millionaire." I read further into the article. "Lives in Fort McMurray, Alberta."

"Yes," Cheryl said. "It's up north. Medium-sized city. He's a big hockey booster and has been trying to get a Western Hockey League team up there for years."

I set the article down.

"Go on," she said. "There's more."

In the other articles I found out that Jonathan Sullivan had been taken to court on five different occasions—mainly fraud charges. But nothing had ever been proven against him.

"Interesting," I said.

"More than interesting. We now have someone who could gain from having you off the team. We now have someone who appears to be the type to play dirty."

"One problem," I said without thinking. "He can't get into our dressing room."

She rolled her eyeballs. "Brian, don't you think he can pay someone?"

So much for being a computer-like hockey player.

"I knew that," I said. "Really."

"Sure." She smiled at me. I could get used to those smiles. "Now, give me your list of people who can get into the dressing room."

77

I passed it across the table.

She hummed to herself as she studied it. "We'll need photographs of each of them."

"Why?"

"You'll see," she said. "Trust me on this."

As if I had a choice.

"Well," I said, "some of them have their photographs in the Rebels' program. You know, the one they sell at games."

"And the others?" she asked.

I shrugged. "Unless you're going to walk up to them and ask them to say cheese . . ."

"Good plan."

I tried to tell her I had meant it as a joke, but she kept talking and I didn't have the chance.

"You'll have to take me to tomorrow night's game," she said.

"I can't," I said. "Somebody will recognize me. I'm supposed to be in Winnipeg for urgent 'personal reasons,' remember?"

She smiled sweetly. "No problem. I'm in the drama club. I'll dress you up in a great disguise."

Sixteen

It felt strange to walk into the Centrium to *watch* a Rebels game rather than play one. It felt even stranger to wear a wig.

"This won't work," I told Cheryl, "not in a million years."

She was in blue jeans and a nice blue jacket, and she carried a heavy black purse.

"Relax," she said, "you look perfect."

Perfect? Cheryl had glued a false mustache into place. My wig had a ponytail, and I was wearing a baseball cap. I wore greasy jeans with holes in the knees and a Harley Davidson T-shirt beneath an unbuttoned red flannel hunting shirt. I had rolled the sleeves up to show the tattoos on my forearms. They were new tattoos, the kind you put on with water. In my shirt pocket I had a package of cigarettes.

"Try to walk more floppy," she said.

"What?" I looked to see if anyone in the crowds around us had heard her. "Floppy?"

"You're walking tight like an athlete," she said. "Headbanger rock-and-roll types don't walk that way. Make your head and arms floppy, and walk with a slouch."

"Like this?" I took a few goofy steps.

Cheryl giggled. "Exactly."

We walked up the steps toward our seats. Halfway up, we met a biker with a leather jacket and long greasy hair.

"Dude," the biker said to me, "got a smoke?"

"Sorry," I said. "I don't smoke. It's bad for your health."

"Cool joke, dude," the guy said. "Like, major irony. Mock the athletes of this world."

I didn't think I had been trying to make a joke until Cheryl kicked my ankle. I remembered the cigarettes in my pocket.

"Hey man," I said as I grabbed the cigarettes, "help yourself."

He took half a dozen cigarettes from the pack and stuck it back in my pocket. Cheryl and I continued up the stairs.

"See what I mean?" Cheryl said. "Perfect."

We sat in section VV, row 22, across from the players' bench. I soaked in the music and the smell of popcorn and the feeling of nervous excitement in the crowd. Cheryl kept turning her head to look in all directions.

"This might be fun," she said. "I feel like a kid at a circus. Maybe I'll come to some more games later."

"Wonderful," I said, not meaning it.

"Only if you're playing."

"That's better."

At the other end of the ice, the Saskatoon Blades were skating circles to warm up. The Blades were usually a powerhouse team, but for some reason had not been playing well lately. We were expected to beat them easily tonight.

I watched the Rebels in our end. My chest tightened to see the guys. Mulridge. Shertzer. Mancini. Hog Burnell. And the rest of the team in the white, gray, and black Rebel uniforms. I had missed hockey bad enough before, but I began to miss it ten times more now. It was killing me to just watch.

"Cheryl," I whispered. "This has got to work. I'll die if it doesn't."

She frowned at me. "Don't be stupid. No matter how much fun hockey is, there are plenty of other things that are more important."

I opened my mouth to defend myself, then changed my mind. She was giving me that kind of frown.

"The list," I said to change the subject. She pulled it out of her purse. The list contained all the people who could get into the dressing room anytime they wanted.

She had asked for everyone, and I had put down everyone, no matter how unlikely. Sam Radisson, the owner. Lucas Turner, general manager. Kurt Doyle, promotions manager. Coach Blair. Assistant Coach Kimball. Teddy the trainer. The stickboys. All the press guys I could remember. I even put down the "Zamboni driver" because he worked maintenance and had a key to all the rooms in the Centrium.

"Hmm," she said as she re-read the list. "Hmm."

"Hmm?"

"I had a chance to speak to Robbie Patterson today," she told me. She was whispering, and I had to lean closer to hear. Her perfume smelled nice.

"Robbie? Our goalie?"

"Yes," she said, "he's in my biology class. I asked him to tell me as much as he could about the dressing room after the second period of the last game."

"Because if someone did something to his glove, it would have been then, right? His glove broke in the third period."

"Right," she said.

I was glad I wasn't so nervous around her any more. It gave me the chance to think.

"Let me guess," I said. "You asked him who besides players were in the dressing room."

"Exactly." She looked at the paper. "That means you can cross everyone off the list except for Kurt Doyle, Coach Blair, Assistant Coach Kimball, Teddy the trainer, and the stickboys."

"Kurt Doyle's photo is in the program. Same with Coach Blair and Kimball. So you won't need to take their photos."

"Stickboys and trainer," she said. "Can you point them out from here?"

I could. I looked across the ice and described what Teddy was wearing. Then I told her what the stickboys were wearing.

"Good," she answered. She patted her purse. "I've got my camera in here. I'll wander over to the other side sometime during the game and take all the photos I need."

"Why?" I asked. It had been hard to hold on to that question as long as I had. "What good will their photos do?"

"Cockroaches," she answered. "If we can find out where the cockroaches came from, we might have our man."

"I don't understand."

"You will tomorrow when you go to Calgary."

"What? Calgary?"

She patted my knee. "Just relax and watch the game. I'll worry about getting the photos. In the meantime, maybe you can explain some of the rules to me."

I did my best.

The game opened with the Rebels scoring two goals in the first two minutes. By the end of the first period we were ahead by five goals. By the end of the second, we were only ahead by three goals. At the end of the game, we won by a single goal in a 10–9 battle that was not very defensive, and I had winced every time a defensive mistake in our end cost us a goal.

Still, it could have been worse. We could have lost. Now we had to win ten games with thirteen to go. And I was hoping I could get back on the ice before it was too late.

Seventeen

After the game, Cheryl and I went to the Dairy Queen downtown. A milkshake for me. Diet cola for her.

"All right," I said as soon as we sat down, "how about finally telling me what the pictures are all about."

"Find the person who put cockroaches in Jason's equipment," she said, "and you'll find the person behind all of the strange things happening to the team."

"Sure," I agreed, "but how do we do that?"

"Go to Biology Supply Importers in Calgary. It's the only company in the entire province of Alberta that sells cockroaches."

Sells cockroaches?

She laughed at the look on my face. "Yes, they sell cockroaches. Alberta has cold winters—it isn't like Mexico where you can find cockroaches anywhere. If you want cockroaches, you'll have a much easier time buying them than trying to capture them. Lucky for us there's only one place that sells them."

"But why would anyone sell cockroaches?"

She dug into her purse and pulled out a small brochure. "I hope this doesn't spoil your appetite," she said.

I moved my straw so that it wouldn't get caught in my false moustache. I was worried some of the guys might stop by after the game, so I was still wearing my disguise. I took a good slurp of the milkshake, then read the brochure.

"What?" I said a few seconds later. "Preserved cats for ten dollars each?"

"Sounds gross, doesn't it? My dad gave this brochure to me. He's the one who suggested we try to track this down through the cockroaches."

Cats weren't the only animals in the brochure. There were frogs, sold by the dozen, snakes, earthworms, grasshoppers, squid, minnows, and monkeys. Some were sold dead, others alive.

"Dead animals and live animals," I said. "What's the deal?"

"For science labs in universities, colleges, and high schools," she explained. "Animals like frogs and snakes and cats to dissect don't just wander into the lab and ask to be experimented on."

I put the straw to my mouth for another gulp of milkshake. I thought of slimy dead squids and changed my mind.

"I think I understand," I said as I set the milkshake aside. "If someone bought the cockroaches to put in Jason's equipment, that person had to buy them from Biology Supply Importers."

"That's the way Dad looked at it too."

"And you think I should go to their office and ask

them if they sold cockroaches to anyone in the last couple of weeks."

"Yes," Cheryl said, "show them all the photographs too. Maybe the person didn't use his real name when he bought them."

"*If* he bought them," I said. "This doesn't sound like a sure thing."

"It isn't a sure thing," she agreed, "but can you think of a better idea?"

I stayed in a motel again that night. I was glad to be able to take the wig and false mustache off, but no matter how hard I scrubbed, the tattoos stayed on my arm.

I fell asleep wondering about the cockroaches. *Sure you could dump a jarful into someone's duffel bag, but how could you get them to bury themselves in all the cracks in a guy's equipment? And how could you get them to not move as Jason got dressed and then move as Jason began to skate? You couldn't inject each cockroach with a sleeping potion and then push it into the equipment. Even if that were possible, how would you know that the cockroaches would wake up at exactly the right time?*

It was too much of a puzzle for me to solve. Thinking of cockroaches didn't help my sleep much, either. I kept dreaming of giant ones chasing me around the ice.

I was tired, then, when I woke up the next morning. The drive south to Calgary took me and my old truck about an hour and a half. I should have enjoyed the view as I drove. The highway is mostly straight and flat, which some people might find boring. But a prairie sky is a pretty picture, with colors from the blue of a robin's egg to the oranges and yellows on sun-streaked clouds. Plus for much of the way to Calgary you can see the jagged edges of Rocky Mountains against the western horizon.

I couldn't enjoy the view, though. I was too nervous, hoping that Cheryl's plan would work. *And what was I going to say once I got to Biology Supply Importers? Could I just march in and demand that they tell me what I wanted to know?*

When I got to Calgary, the first thing I did was stop by a one-hour photo shop to get Cheryl's film developed. There were photos of the stickboys and of Teddy the trainer. There were also some photos of Cheryl and me together, making goofy faces into the camera as I had held it in my hand and pointed it toward us. I sure looked weird in the ponytail wig, but she was pretty, even with her tongue sticking out.

After leaving the photo shop, it took me a half hour to find Biology Supply Importers at a small warehouse in the southeast part of Calgary. Not until I pulled into the parking lot had I decided how I would approach this. With honesty.

"Hello," I said as I walked into a tiny office to see a woman at a desk. She was an older lady with hair dyed an unusual shade of red. She looked up from the *Calgary Sun* newspaper in her hands.

"Hello, sugar," she said. She was chewing gum and grinning at me. "What's a handsome guy like you doing in a place like this?"

I stared at the floor and tried to figure out what to say to *that.*

She laughed. "Don't worry, sunshine. I'm just trying to have fun. You can't imagine what it's like answering the phone and taking orders for tarantulas or chimpanzees or squid."

"How about cockroaches?" I asked.

"Cockroaches? You want cockroaches. Dead or alive? Of course, they're so tough to kill, I'll bet half the dead ones are still kicking by the time they get here."

I tried not to think of how they had been crawling on Jason's belly just before he fainted.

"Actually," I said, "I wonder if you can tell me if you've sold any in the last couple of weeks."

She stopped popping her gum and gave me a hard look. "That's not information I would usually give out."

"Ma'am," I said, "someone played a nasty joke on a friend of mine. I've also been a target of some mean jokes. If I can find out who did them, the pranks might end."

She lifted a cup of coffee from her messy desk. She took a gulp. "How do these jokes involve cockroaches?"

I told her how Jason had ripped off his hockey equipment at the beginning of the game against the Lethbridge Hurricanes.

The woman laughed so hard that she began to cough. To stop her coughing, she lit a cigarette. "That's a good story, sunshine. Good enough that I'll do you a favor."

She tapped the side of her head with her index finger, showing shiny, dark purple nail polish.

"I don't forget anything," she said, tapping her head again. "A mind like a steel trap. And it was less than two weeks ago I got an order for live cockroaches."

"Really!" I couldn't believe this was actually working.

"Yup. A Sam Jones. Came by to pick them up himself."

"Oh," I said. Maybe this wasn't going to work. "Where was he from?"

"He didn't say."

I had a Red Deer Rebels' game program folded to fit in my back pocket. I pointed out the photos of Kurt Doyle, Coach Blair, and Assistant Coach Kimball.

She shook her head no. "Wasn't any of them."

I pointed at Kimball's photo. "You're sure it wasn't him?"

She popped another bubble and shook her head. "Weren't him."

I lost all hope. If it wasn't Kimball, I couldn't understand who it might be. I took out the envelope of photos. "Could you look through these?" I asked.

She went through the photos. "Nice-looking girl," she said. "Why would she hang out with a long-haired goofball like that?"

"What?" Then I remembered the photos of Cheryl and me in the package. "Um, it's a long story."

"Must be," the redhaired woman said. She stopped and frowned. "Hey, this is Sam Jones right here."

My heart bounced around a few times.

"No way!" I said.

"Yes way." She popped a bubble. She pulled a photograph out of the pile and handed it to me.

I couldn't believe what I saw. "Are you sure?" I asked.

"Absitively," she said. "Posilutely. This is one old girl who don't ever make mistakes when it comes to faces."

I still didn't want to believe her. But it looked like I had no choice. My next problem was what to do about it.

Eighteen

I made it back to Red Deer that afternoon well before the three o'clock team practice. I sat in my truck in the nearly empty parking lot of the Centrium for almost ten minutes, trying to work up the courage to go inside. I wasn't good at asking people for help. But it seemed all I could do. So I took a deep breath and stepped out of the truck.

A cool March breeze brushed my face as I walked toward the side doors of the building. I was walking without my duffel bag of hockey equipment. I had left the bag in the back of the truck. If my plan worked, I would come out again soon to get it. If my plan didn't work, I might never need the equipment again.

I found Coach Blair sitting in his office, going over the practice schedule. He was surprised to see me in the doorway.

"McPhee," he said. "I thought—"

"Coach, you told me our team needed to stick together." On the drive back from Calgary, I had memorized what I wanted to say, and I was afraid if I let Coach Blair interrupt me, I might not get the words out right. "You told me if all the guys couldn't trust someone on the team, it wouldn't be much of a team."

"Yes, but—"

"Coach, what if I could get them to trust me? Could I play?"

"B. T.," he said, "I understand what you're going through. Really. And I wish you were back on the team. We need you on the blue line. But every one of them is convinced you stole the wallets. I don't see how you can change their minds."

"Will you give me a chance?" I asked.

He thought for several seconds. "Everyone deserves a chance," he said slowly. "We'll go to the dressing room right now. Tell them what you want to say. Then I'll put it to a team vote."

"Thank you," I said. And I meant it. "There is one thing, though."

He frowned. "One thing?"

"Can you find a way to make sure Teddy doesn't know about this?"

"Teddy? Our trainer? I don't understand."

"It's really important," I said. I took a deep breath. "He put the cockroaches in Jason's equipment. I think it means he's the one who put the wallets in my duffel bag."

Coach Blair's frown deepened. "You'd better have

a good reason to say something like that. Explain yourself."

I did. From the beginning.

The dressing room became very quiet when the guys realized I had walked in behind Coach Blair. Too quiet.

Nothing else had changed. Practice jerseys piled in one corner, lockers half-open, sticks everywhere. The smell of old sweat and new sweat and sharp spearmint ointment.

"Hi, guys," I said.

"Come to give us our money back?" Mancini asked. "Or were you hoping we'd left our wallets out for you to steal again?"

"Give him a break," Hog Burnell called out.

"Thanks, Hog." I hoped my voice wasn't shaking as badly as my knees.

"Listen up," Coach Blair said. "I've sent Teddy out to get pizzas. I told him it would be a reward for you guys at the end of practice. But I had another reason."

Coach Blair looked around the room. "I don't want Teddy to know about this. I want you guys to listen to McPhee. If you decide he's not a thief, he's back on the team."

Coach Blair moved to the nearest bench and sat down. "Go ahead, B. T.," he said. "Tell them what you told me."

I was the only person standing. All eyes were on me. I probably spoke too fast, and I know I didn't say everything the way I had planned it. By the time I finished, though, I had managed to explain most of it.

"The woman at Biology Supply Importers pointed to Teddy's photo," I finished. "He bought live cockroaches just before that game against the Hurricanes. I think chances are pretty good he's the guy who did it. And if he did the cockroaches, I think he's behind all the other things I just told you about."

"I don't get it," Jason said. "I've never done anything to him."

"He wasn't trying to get you. I think he was trying to get at the team."

"But why?" Hog asked.

"There's a businessman who wants to buy the team. You guys remember that from the newspapers?"

Most of the guys nodded.

"If we don't make the playoffs," I said, "the team won't be worth as much. He could buy it for a lot less and save himself a pile of money. All I can figure is Teddy is working for the man."

Hog Burnell stood. He was wearing most of his equipment, and he had his skates on, unlaced.

"Either McPhee is the best liar in the world, or we ought to believe him," Hog said. "McPhee wasn't here when Robbie's glove snapped. McPhee wouldn't take a rivet out of his own skate. And I don't think McPhee's so stupid he would steal our wallets and leave them in his duffel bag."

Hog paused for breath. I'd never heard him talk this much. "What I'm saying," Hog went on, "is I'm glad there seems to be a reason those wallets were stuck in his duffel bag. I didn't want to believe McPhee stole them. And I'd like McPhee and his stupid, ugly face back for the rest of the season."

"Me too," Mancini said. "I'm sorry, McPhee. I shouldn't have shot my mouth off."

"Stick to shooting pucks," Jason said to Mancini. "You couldn't hurt a flea that way."

The rest of the guys hooted at the insult. Right then, because no one seemed angry or upset, I knew I'd be back on the team.

"Anyone think McPhee doesn't belong here?" Coach Blair yelled above the laughing.

Not a single person raised a hand.

Coach Blair stood and walked over to shake my hand. "Welcome back," he said.

"Thank you. I missed this big time."

"What about Teddy?" Jason asked. "I'm not real happy about those cockroaches."

Coach Blair faced the rest of the team. "I'm going to have a long talk with him. If he doesn't have a good explanation for those cockroaches, you won't have to worry about him for the rest of the season."

Nineteen

Coach Blair told us later that Teddy didn't deny the cockroaches. But Teddy didn't say anything else about them or his other stunts against the team. He just announced he was quitting and walked out of Coach Blair's office. While we didn't learn anything more, at least I had been proven innocent. I went back to boarding at the Henrys after telling them the whole story. They seemed relieved.

By then, however, Teddy had come very close to doing all the damage he needed. After all, I got back onto the team with only thirteen games left in the regular season. We had to win ten of them to make the playoffs. The odds were greatly against us, and Teddy probably thought he had already done enough to keep us out of the playoffs.

We proved him wrong though.

I think it happened because we were so angry that someone had tried to make us lose through dirty tricks.

Every time we stepped on the ice for a new game, we played like we were fighting an invasion.

On the road, we beat the Spokane Chiefs 5–3. Continuing our run south, we went into Portland and hammered the Winter Hawks 9–2. We went up to Seattle and tied the Thunderbirds at 5 goals each, following it up with another tie—this one 3–3—against the Tacoma Rockets. Our trip into the northwestern states netted us two wins and two ties, equal to three wins in four games.

It left us needing seven wins out of our last nine games. Tough odds, but we were still mad, and we had never played better.

Swinging east of Red Deer into the prairie province of Saskatchewan, we stopped in Moose Jaw and tore the Warriors apart, 10–1. In Regina, we hit the Pats harder than we'd hit them all season. Our reward against them was a 7–5 victory. From Regina we traveled north again, and we beat the Saskatoon Blades 6–3.

Now we were down to six games, but we only needed four wins. We made the mistake of thinking we were already there, because we relaxed when the Tri-City Americans played us in Red Deer. The result? A 5–2 loss in front of a sold out hometown crowd.

With five games left, we still needed four wins.

We tied the Prince Alberta Raiders at 4–4, then tied our next game 2–2 against the visiting Kamloops Blazers. Two ties were worth one win. Three games left, but we needed three wins.

Could we do it?

We thought so. The next two games were on the road. First we'd go down to Medicine Hat to play the Tigers, then to Lethbridge to face the Hurricanes. Our final game would be back in Red Deer, again against the Hurricanes.

We had a two-day break before playing Medicine Hat, and it showed in the energy we had on the ice. Against the Tigers, we busted into a four-goal lead by the end of the first period and stayed in front all the way, finishing with the same four-goal lead at 7–3.

That left us with two games against the Hurricanes. The first one in Lethbridge. The last one at home in Red Deer. We had to win both games. If the Hurricanes managed to beat us once, or even tie us once, they would make the playoffs. And we would be out.

Sometimes games are won or lost on good breaks or bad breaks. We won the first game against the Hurricanes because of good breaks. They rang five shots off the goal posts in the third period. Five shots so close to scoring that had even one of those shots bounced toward the net instead of away, we would have been shut out of the playoffs. Instead, we barely managed to stay alive, and we beat them in overtime, 4–3.

Our entire season, then, came down to the final game against the Lethbridge Hurricanes. Whoever won would go to the playoffs.

I wondered if Teddy might try something to make us lose.

Twenty

I'm nervous about tonight's game," I told Cheryl right after English class, "real nervous."

Standing together in the crowded school hallway, Cheryl and I were a small island with streams of kids flowing around us. The noise of clanging locker doors and shouting and laughing students filled the hall.

"Nervous? Brian, you're playing the best hockey of your life. So is the team. And now that Teddy is gone, he won't be able to do anything to hurt you guys."

"I'm still nervous," I said.

Cheryl grinned at me. "Be a big boy. Get over it."

"Get over it?" I said. "Get over it? It's not that easy. If we lose or tie, we don't make the playoffs."

"And what's your point?"

It still seemed like every time I looked at Cheryl my heart flip-flopped like I was seeing her for the first time. I wanted to tell her that. I wanted to tell her how important it was that she and I were friends. But I couldn't.

If she knew how much I cared, she would be able to hurt me. I couldn't allow myself the risk.

Instead of telling her what was going through my mind as I watched her smile, I said, "My point? I've told you how I worry and worry about making mistakes during a big game. I'm afraid tonight will be the game where I fold under pressure."

"Come on," she said. "Let's go outside where it's quiet."

"We'll be late for our classes."

"Worse things have happened," she said.

She took me by the hand and pulled me through the swarms of kids in the hall. I didn't know if this was good or bad. Cheryl never skipped classes, never showed up late.

We went through the doors at the end of the hallway and stepped into mid-morning sunshine.

We had the steps and the spring sunshine to ourselves. She didn't let go of my hand. Nor did she waste any time.

"Brian Thomas McPhee," she said, "I don't like listening to speeches and I don't like making speeches. But you're stuck with this one anyway."

"Why?"

"Because you are officially my favorite guy." She studied my face. "Come on, smile. I hope that wasn't bad news."

"It's great news," I said. I found myself staring at the ground because I suddenly felt shy. So when she gave me a hug, it was a surprise. A nice surprise.

She stepped back. "Now for my speech."

I waited.

"Remember the game you wore a ponytail wig?"

I nodded. "The tattoos still haven't come off my arms. The guys bug me about them all the time."

She gave me a quick smile, but got serious again. "Remember when you said you would die if my plan didn't work and you couldn't play hockey?"

I nodded again. I also remembered the strange look she had given me when I said it.

"Remember that I told you no matter how much fun hockey is, there are plenty of things more important?" She poked me in the chest. "I'm going to get mad at you if you didn't learn anything in the last month."

"Sure. Lots."

"Like what?"

"Like I'm glad to be playing hockey again."

Wrong thing to say. Thunderclouds of anger covered her face.

"Listen, McPhee, I don't care how good a player you are, if hockey is all you have in your life, you're a loser. A serious loser."

"But—"

"But nothing." She was steamed and not afraid to show it. "Maybe next time it's an injury that puts you out of hockey. And, even if you actually get through an entire hockey career, you'll have to retire someday. Either way, you won't be a hockey player the rest of your life."

"But—"

"I'm not finished. You can't let your happiness depend

on how you're playing hockey. Because when hockey goes, so does your happiness. And you can bet sooner or later there will come a day when hockey goes."

I was beginning to understand. When I thought I'd been kicked out of hockey, I had been miserable.

"Instead," she went on, "build yourself a life. Friends, family, and faith in God are things that are *really* important. Develop other interests, too. Become someone other people want to be with. When hockey works for you, great; it's a bonus. If hockey doesn't work, you won't be destroyed because you'll have all the other stuff to fall back on."

I opened my mouth to say something, but she didn't let me.

"Maybe it's part of those walls you build around yourself. Maybe if you relaxed, the walls wouldn't be so important. Like with your mom. Your face looks so hurt every time you talk about her, but you won't even let her talk to you. Maybe she regrets what she did. Help her out and give her a chance."

"Just a second—"

"Look," she said, "if hockey becomes fun for you instead of a matter of life or death, you won't be so scared of playing badly. And I'll bet when you're not scared of playing bad hockey, it's going to be a lot easier for you to play good hockey. And when you're having fun with hockey, maybe you won't have to be so serious with everything else."

I tried one more time to say something, but again I was helpless as she kept going full speed.

"Someday you're going to be an old man, and you'll have the memories of your games. Instead of being afraid on the ice, why don't you try to enjoy it as much as possible, for the days when you look back and miss hockey?"

She took both my hands in her hands and her frown became a smile. "If you don't believe anything I just said, I hope you'll believe this last part. You're my official favorite guy because you're you. Not because you're a hockey star."

With that, she stepped onto her tiptoes and kissed me briefly on my cheek, then marched away from me and back into the school.

I stood there as stunned as if someone had slammed me with a body check into the boards. She had gone from warm and friendly to really mad to giving me a kiss. All in under two minutes.

Women.

Twenty-One

I stood on the blue line, waiting for the ref to drop the puck to start the game. The roaring of the crowd in the Centrium seemed to become part of the blood pumping through my heart. I began to understand some of what Cheryl had told me. This was an incredibly exciting moment. Instead of feeling fear, I should be soaking in this excitement and trying to hold on to the memory of it forever.

As I began to understand, I felt like a stone shell around me began to crack. If I didn't spend so much time holding onto my worries, I could actually enjoy this. The skating at full speed, the concentration of trying to make a good pass, the joy of giving it absolutely everything I had.

I grinned and waited for the puck to drop. *Let's get this one going boys. I'm ready.*

The puck dropped. Mancini picked it out of the air and knocked it back to me. The Hurricane winger rushed in. I faked a pass across to Jason. It froze the winger briefly, long enough to let me push right and around him.

That gave me a few seconds of clear ice. I raced ahead with the puck and dished it off to Burnell just as the center rushed toward me.

Burnell took it in across their blue line. I had momentum going and instead of hitting the brakes, I followed the play, making sure our other winger Louie Shertzer had dropped back to cover my position on defense.

Burnell barreled around their defenseman, and I busted straight to the net. I didn't care how many guys I had to take out to get there, but they were going to pay the price for getting in my way.

The other defenseman elbowed me in the ribs then wrapped his arms around me. We fell in a heap and went sliding toward the net.

Something bounced off my helmet. I thought it was a stick blade until the roar of the crowd exploded like a jet taking off.

A goal! Not a stick blade off my helmet, but a puck! Burnell had dropped the puck back to Mancini, and Mancini had fired a low screamer that had deflected off my helmet into the top corner of the net. First shift and a goal!

I rose, screaming and jumping. Two guys pounded my back. *So this was hockey without fear. I could learn to like it all right.*

Next shift I managed to stop a sure breakaway for the Hurricanes by intercepting a long pass up the middle to their center. I cradled the puck with my stick and took two steps forward before firing a slap shot around the boards into the Hurricane end.

Three shifts later I bodychecked their biggest forward so hard we were able to hear him slam into the boards above the roaring of the crowd.

I was on fire. The rest of the Rebels were on fire. For the first ten minutes of the first period, we fought for position in their end like bears clawing for honey. We came away with another two goals.

With nine minutes left in the first period, and a 3–0 lead, we looked unstoppable.

Then, suddenly, our passes in their end began to bounce and tumble instead of slide across the ice with smooth precision. We lost a bit of our zip. Instead of beating their defensemen to the puck, it seemed like we were skating uphill.

Slowly, the game began to turn in their direction.

When they crossed the line at center ice, the Hurricane forwards had all the speed we had lost in their end. Their passes were slick and quicker than bullets. Jason and I scrambled just to stay in position against their furious attacks. Against our second line, the Hurricanes scored two quick goals, and we felt lucky to survive the final four minutes of the period without giving up any more points.

The first period ended with us ahead by only one goal—3–2—and with the crowd much too quiet. It looked like we were going to fold during the biggest game of our season.

Our dressing room, too, was quiet during the break between the first and second period. Coach Blair only spoke once during the entire break. He spoke quietly and worry lines made him appear much older. I understood. His job depended on this game.

"This one is yours if you want it boys," Coach Blair said. "Skate like you did the first half of that period, and we'll be in the playoffs."

We took his advice.

We opened the second period exactly the way we opened the first period. In control.

The teams had switched ends for the second period. The Hurricanes now defended the half of the ice we had been defending in the first period. We defended the other end.

Switching ends seemed to improve our luck. When we attacked the Hurricanes, our passes were bullets again, sliding slick and fast along the ice.

Better yet, the Hurricanes struggled during their attack against us, just like we'd struggled against them when they were defending the net in our end during the first period.

We scored another goal in the first five minutes, going ahead 4–2.

Then, unbelievably, the game began to slowly turn against us again. Our passes lost their zip, and it was a killer to try to skate fast through their end. As we began to get worse, they began to get better. I took a tripping penalty trying to stop their center, and the Hurricanes scored during their power play. Next shift, they scored again, on a long shot from the point*.

Tied 4–4, with twelve minutes left in the second period, we were fading fast. We couldn't seem to get anything right in the Hurricane end. But they were getting everything right in our end.

I was sitting on our players' bench, gasping for breath and watching the second line struggle against the Hurricanes, when I heard a familiar voice call my name.

I looked behind me into the crowd. Cheryl was at the side of the Plexiglas that protected our players' box. The same Plexiglas that someone had leaned over to dump cola on me a few weeks earlier.

Only Cheryl wasn't ready to dump a drink. Instead, she flipped a crumpled ball of paper over the Plexiglas. It landed in my lap.

I couldn't shout and ask her what it was about. She was already moving away, and I was supposed to be concentrating on the game.

I shook my hockey gloves off my hands and opened the paper. Drops of sweat fell from my nose and blotted the ink of her neat handwriting.

I saw Teddy here. I followed him after the first period. He spent some time in a locked room underneath the stands at the back of the arena. Does this mean anything?

I didn't have time to wonder.

Jewels Larken, our backup goaltender, was screaming for me to hit the ice. I did as our team changed players on the go. The Hurricanes zoomed into our end at full speed, passing the puck back and forth like it was a ball on the end of a string.

We fought and scrambled to stop them, but their speed was too much. Thirty seconds later, the crowd moaned as the puck zinged into our net. Now we were down 5–4 and playing so badly I wondered if we would ever move the puck into their end again.

"Man," Hog said as we slowly returned to the players' bench, "I can't get nowhere against their defense. It's like skating through glue."

"I wish we had that problem in our end," I said. "It's like a sheet of glass for the Hurricanes."

Then it hit me. *Skating through glue in the Hurricanes' end. Skating like glass in our end. And Teddy spending time in a locked room underneath the stands at the back of the Centrium.*

As I stepped into the players' box, I waved for Coach Blair to move toward me.

"Can you call a time-out?" I said to him. "I think I know why we're losing. And I think I know how to stop it."

Twenty-Two

The Hurricanes scored once more, and we left the ice down 6–4 at the end of the second period. I had never heard our dressing room so quiet. Most of the guys stared at the floor. For a full five minutes, not one single word was said.

Hog Burnell broke the silence by firing a couple questions at me. "B. T., what did you say to Coach Blair during the time-out? And where did Coach Blair go at the end of the period?"

How could I explain to Hog that I had a crazy theory and that Coach Blair and security guards were checking it out as we waited here?

"Did any of you guys find the ice real strange?" I answered. "Like slow in the Hurricanes' end and fast in ours?"

"I did," Mancini said. "Man, I couldn't get anywhere in their end. And every time I tried to pass, the puck stuck or bounced."

I nodded. "Soft ice."

"Not in our end," Jason said. "Their wingers were killing us."

"Well," I told them all, "Teddy was here tonight. This may sound stupid, but I think he was—"

The dressing room door opened and Coach Blair stepped inside.

"We got Teddy," Coach Blair said to me. "Red-handed. Exactly where you said he would be. And doing exactly what you guessed."

Coach Blair looked at his watch. "I want to tell all of you what happened. And when I'm finished, I want you to go out there and take it to the Hurricanes. Under fair conditions."

"Fair?" Mancini echoed.

"You guys know the ice is made over a layer of refrigerated pipes," Coach Blair said. "Well, Teddy had stolen a set of maintenance keys. He could get into any room in this building, including the control room for the ice. That's where we caught him less than five minutes ago."

"In the control room?" Hog said.

"In the control room. Teddy was doing his best to make sure we lost."

"But how?" Mancini asked. His eyes widened as he figured out the same thing I had earlier. "I know! Slow ice and fast ice!"

"Exactly," Coach Blair told him. "At the beginning of the first period, he adjusted the temperature of the pipes in the Lethbridge end to make it slower. He made it faster in our end."

That explained it all right. The temperature change wouldn't be instant. It would take time. Like about half a period. In the beginning of the game, we had come out skating and passing until halfway through the period, the ice had begun to warm up and slow us down. While in our end, it became easier for the Hurricanes to skate and pass the puck on colder, harder ice.

"During the break after the first period," Coach Blair said, "he went back in and reversed the settings."

That explained the second period. We had switched ends with the Hurricanes, and Teddy needed to make the other side of the ice slow. Again, it took about a half period.

"We figured he'd go back in again after the second period to switch temperatures for when we switched ends in the third period," Coach Blair said. He smiled at me. "Correction. *We* didn't figure it. Actually, B. T. guessed it."

"I had help," I told everyone.

"From the cute blonde who put those tattoos on your arms?" Jason asked. "The one who threw you a note? We were betting it was a love note."

I changed the subject. "Coach Blair, did Teddy explain why he was doing all this?"

"Yup. And you were right about that too. Teddy has a gambling problem and owes tens of thousands of dollars. He was so desperate, he hired on with the businessman from Fort McMurray who wanted to drive the price of the team down. Teddy is willing to testify in court, and it looks like the guy will get nailed."

"Teddy was behind everything, right?" I asked.

Coach Blair confirmed that, too. "Teddy even had a friend dump cola on you, B.T. Teddy figured if he could mess up your game, he'd have a good chance of messing up the Rebels."

"What about me?" Jason said. He shivered. "Those stupid cockroaches."

"Bad break for you," Coach Blair said. "Teddy thought he was dumping them in B. T.'s duffel bag. Remember one of your numbers fell off? Teddy wanted to put the cockroaches in B. T.'s bag—number 3—but put them in number 33 by mistake because one of the threes was missing. He said that's what gave him the idea of switching your bags around later so you could find the wallets in B. T.'s duffel bag."

"But Coach," I said. "Jason should have been able to see the cockroaches as soon as he opened the duffel bag."

"Road trip," Coach Blair said. "Teddy said he dumped them in the duffel bag just before he threw the equipment on the bus. The luggage compartment of the bus is unheated. We spent three and a half hours on the road. As the equipment got colder and colder, the cockroaches must have burrowed into the cracks of Jason's equipment. And naturally, half-frozen, they wouldn't have started to crawl around until Jason had warmed them up by skating around before the game."

Jason groaned.

"Teddy was proud of that one," Coach said. "He remembered something like that happening to a teammate. They practiced in an old, wooden arena, and they didn't know the dressing room was infested with cockroaches." Coach Blair laughed. "Sorry, Jason. But it was a funny story. The cockroaches had nested in someone's equipment, and the guy didn't find out until he was skating on the ice. He peeled his equipment off right then and there too. Of course, for the other guy it was just a practice."

Jason kept groaning.

"Teddy was just trying to throw you guys off your games. He figured even if you found the cockroaches before you dressed, it would have done that. In fact, he intended to keep doing these little things, hoping to get you guys from thinking hockey."

"Flat tires?" I asked. "Fiberglass? Skate rivets? Everything?"

"Yup. Yup. Yup. And yup. Does that make any of you guys angry?"

We all roared, filling the dressing room with our shouts of anger.

"Good," Coach Blair said when we stopped yelling. "The law will take care of Teddy and the guy who hired him. You guys just need to worry about beating the Hurricanes. Get out there and show that anger in this final period."

Twenty-Three

We came out storming. Five minutes into the third period, we had already taken nearly a dozen shots on their net. Two were mine—a slap shot that dinged the crossbar of the net, and a wrist shot from the top of the faceoff circle that the Hurricane goalie barely managed to knock aside with his blocker.

As a team, I think we could sense the game was ours if we just pushed a little harder. Our first break happened two minutes later. I hit Mancini up the middle with a pass, and he and Burnell broke free for a two-on-one against their remaining defenseman. Mancini faked a pass over to Burnell and flicked a shot to the right side of the net. It bounced off the post, almost to Burnell's stick, and the defenseman dove into Burnell to keep him from shooting. The result was a two-minute penalty. Jason scored on a slap shot from the blue line less than twenty seconds into our power play.

It left us down by only one goal, 6–5.

Our second break was even better than the first. On the next shift, Jason dumped the puck in around the boards. The Hurricane goalie stepped behind his net to block the puck. But it hopped over his stick and continued around the boards to the other side. Burnell was there. He knocked their defenseman off the puck, took a step toward the faceoff circle and took advantage of the wide open net with a powerful wrist shot in the top right corner.

Six to six!

I was screaming as loud as anyone in the stands.

The Hurricanes dug in. For the next ten minutes, they bumped and checked us into a stalemate. The clock ticked down to the final three minutes of the game.

Down to two minutes. Down to one minute.

Then down to the buzzer, which ended regulation time. Sixty minutes of hockey finished. Ten minutes of overtime remained. If the Hurricanes could keep us from scoring, if the game ended in a tie, the Hurricanes would get that last playoff spot. We would be out.

This time when we filed into the dressing room, the air was filled with shouts.

Coach Blair raised his voice. "What a comeback!" he shouted. "Boys, I'm all out of fingernails. Let's end this overtime real quick, before I chew my fingers down to the bone!"

We responded with loud cheers.

I sat on the bench, smiling at players around me, saying little but trying to enjoy the moment. It was a lot more fun than worrying about making a mistake in overtime.

When the buzzer called us back to the ice, I was ready. So were all the Rebels.

Unfortunately, so were the Hurricanes. They stalemated us as badly as they had for the last half of the third period. The seconds on the game clock drained like sand from an hourglass, and we couldn't do anything to stop the flow of time.

Again, down to three minutes—maybe the final three minutes of our season. For some of us, it could even be the final three minutes of our junior hockey careers.

The crowd screamed in frenzy, and we pushed the Hurricanes hard. But we couldn't score.

Down to two minutes. Down to one minute.

With forty-five seconds on the game clock, I took the puck over the center line and fired it into the Hurricanes' end. Shertzer skated in on the Hurricane defenseman so fast the defenseman's only choice was to fire a slap shot all the way down the ice.

That meant an icing call, which meant a faceoff in the Hurricanes' end. Which meant Coach Blair pulled our goalie. We had an empty net at our back and six skaters to attack the Hurricanes.

Mancini lost the draw. The Hurricane defenseman took the puck behind his net and came out the other side. He was desperate to get the puck out of their end, and he pulled his stick back to pound a high slap shot into the open air between Jason and me as we guarded the blue line.

Probably because I had stopped being afraid, I had one of those moments when instinct takes over. I found myself moving the right direction at the right time without thinking about the what and why of my actions. I was off my feet and diving like a shortstop almost before the puck left the Hurricane defenseman's stick.

Jason told me later I was almost waist-high off ice, stretched out completely flat, my stick ahead of me as far as I could reach.

I was not aware of my position or of how I looked. My eyes were on the puck and I was straining to reach it. In one of the sweetest moments of all the hockey I'd played, I managed to knock the puck down with the blade of my stick.

I thumped back to the ice, and my dive took me in a heavy slide toward Jason. But the puck stopped, wobbling on the blue line. Our sixth man, Burnell, managed to reach it before a Hurricane forward, and he flipped it to Mancini.

Although I was still in a face-first body slide, moving away from the play, I turned my head to watch.

Mancini fired the puck across to Shertzer.

I slid into Jason.

Shertzer took the pass in his skates, kicked it ahead to his stick, and slammed the puck between the leg pads of the surprised goalie.

Jason tumbled on top of me. His skates kicked my shoulder and his full weight knocked the breath out of me. The pain didn't matter.

We'd scored.

Sudden-death overtime and we had scored the goal to end the game! We'd scored the goal it took to begin our playoff race!

Within seconds, I was part of the mob around Shertzer and Mancini. The crowd was so loud, I couldn't hear a word, not even my own shouts.

The rest of the team flooded out of the players' bench to join us in our celebration. Coach Blair and Assistant Coach Kimball trotted across the ice to where we were jumping and screaming and pounding each other's backs.

Coach Blair waded into our celebration. He managed to get close enough to me to grab my hand and shake it.

"Thanks, McPhee," he said.

I just grinned. He didn't owe me anything.

I knew I owed someone though. I owed her for support and help. She was up in the stands somewhere, and I'd be looking for her smile as we skated off the ice.

I'd have to tell her how I had learned what she meant about the importance of hockey. How I had lost the fear and found the fun. And how I'd try to be less afraid of other things too. Like my mom. Or like liking Cheryl or even letting her know how much I liked her.

But I wasn't sure how much of all of this I'd tell her tonight over milkshakes. A guy can't just rush into these things.

Lightning on Ice Series

Rebel Glory

B. T. McPhee, the star defenseman of the Red Deer Rebels, likes his chances of making it as a pro. But he doesn't like the small "accidents" that may keep his team from making the playoffs—and keep him off the team. In the spotlight of high-pressure hockey, B. T. has no choice. Unless he can unravel the mystery, the team's season—and his own career—will surely end. (ISBN 0-8499-3637-3)

All-Star Pride

Hog Burnell is playing on a WHL All-Star Team touring Russia. The goal is to beat the Russian All-Stars in the best-of-seven series to be shown as a television special. Hog could use the money that will come with a series win by the WHL All-Stars. But it doesn't take Hog long to discover there's plenty more money to be made along the way . . . if he's willing to pay the price for it. (ISBN 0-8499-3638-1)

Thunderbird Spirit

Justin Ghostkeeper plays for the Seattle Thunderbirds. He's fast and smooth with a shot as deadly as most pros. Unfortunately, there are more than a few unwilling to accept this full-blooded Cree Indian in hockey. For Mike "Crazy" Keats, haunted by a troubled background that fast makes him friends with Ghostkeeper, it means hockey just got more complicated. The spin-off racial hatred takes him and Justin into a web of violence and deceit that makes winning this year's championship the least of their concerns.
(ISBN 0-8499-3639-X;

Winter Hawk Star

Riley Judd is a star center for the Portland Winter Hawks. His great playing skills are exceeded only by his oversized ego. And that's why he spends more time benched than he does playing. Given the choice of working with street kids in roller hockey or getting kicked off the team, Judd takes what he thinks is the easy way out. But he soon discovers that it could cost him his life to give the kids the help they really need.
(ISBN 0-8499-3640-3;

Western Hockey League

The Western Hockey League
Encourages You to Stay in School

The players of the Western Hockey League are working hard toward reaching the dream of playing in the National Hockey League.

That's not the only thing they are working hard at. They know that as hard as they work on the ice, it is important to work just as hard in the classroom. Education makes them better players and better people.

The Western Hockey League makes sure that all of its players have the opportunity to succeed all the way through high school and into college or university. Players work together with their teachers, counselors, and their teams to learn both on and off the ice.

WHL players know when the going gets tough, on or off the ice, you must never give up. A good education will help you make better decisions about what to do with the puck, or what to do in life situations.

Whenever you have a question or a problem in school, ask your teacher or your counselor for help. And no matter what, STAY IN SCHOOL.